Date Due

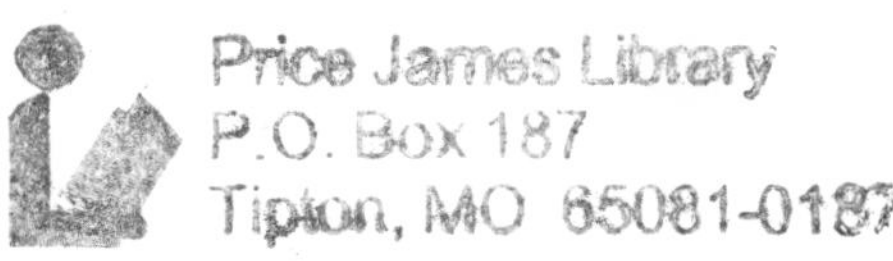

Pinkerton & Friends

A Steven Kellogg Treasury

with an introduction by Helen Hunt
and an afterword by Barbara Elleman

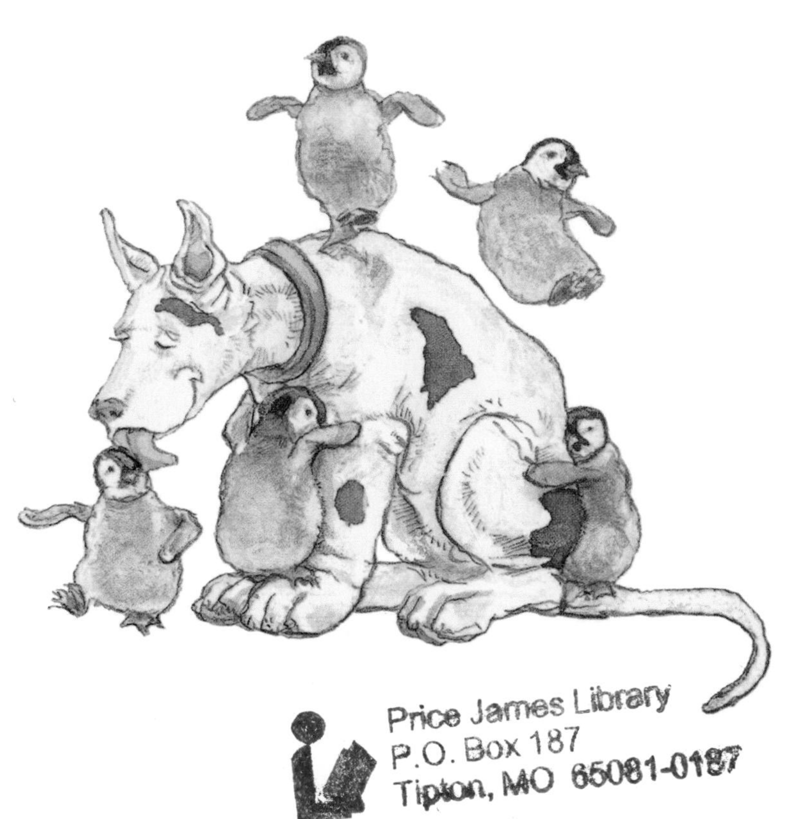

Dial Books for Young Readers  New York

*To Helen and the rest of my wonderful family,
with appreciation and love*

Published by Dial Books for Young Readers
A division of Penguin Young Readers Group
345 Hudson Street, New York, New York 10014

Photo credits: Steven and Helen Kellogg with Pinkerton by Joy Cooley; Steven Kellogg in his studio by Gordon Hunt; Steven Kellogg with Pinkerton by Tom Crider; Dallas Children's Theater cast by Robin Sachs; Steven Kellogg with Goldensilverwind by Michael Duffy

Text set in Galliard
Designed by Lily Malcom
Manufactured in the U.S.A.
ISBN 0-8037-2979-0

Contents

Introduction

I'm tired of feeling small. There, I said it. I'm an adult, by any standard, and I'm *still* tired of feeling small.

I'm also tired of feeling big, but I'll get to that in a minute.

I was the younger of two, and when we went, as we often did, to Sandy Hook, Connecticut, to visit our extended family, the Kelloggs, I became smaller still. Joining Helen and Steve's six kids, that ranked me the smallest of eight. With their enormous Great Dane, Pinkerton, thrown into the mix (you've heard of him), I got smaller still. So there I was, shrinking and shrinking.

And yet . . .

Around Steve, I never felt small, or at least not too small. I felt seen and understood, treasured and delighted.

I remember few things delighting me more as a child than getting to go into Steve's studio. Ochres and crimsons overflowing out of tubes and onto little palettes and putty knives. Seeing *Can I Keep Him?* half finished. Knowing, even incomplete, that it was the truest book anybody ever made. In addition to the various dogs and cats I told my parents I couldn't live without, I believe I met a dolphin at a sea park in Florida when I was six and made a very convincing case for our keeping him too.

But rereading the books that are included in this treasury made me feel another truth about Steve's work and about myself. I still feel small.

Smaller than whatever person I've decided is bigger than I am, smaller than a world filled with enormous forces none of us know how to handle, where Valdoons and Pepperwills fight with no end in sight. Smaller than the personal challenges I've been handed to work through in my life. But in every one of Steve's books, as its narrative is driving along, and its pictures are exploding with color and magic, there is room at its heart for the person who's too small.

Take *Much Bigger Than Martin.* As a child, it is comforting to read about the adventures of another younger sibling, but it's not just that. It's comforting because Henry is mad, Henry is desperate, Henry wants revenge. Henry is *human.*

Or in *Best Friends.* It's not just that Kathy and Louise are friends, or that they are separated and miss each other. It's that Kathy is lost, enraged, punishing. She wishes for "volcanic eruptions" to "blast" her friend's summer retreat "into pebbles." She prays for fifty new friends to replace Louise, while vowing to keep every puppy in the world out of her reach.

Henry and Louise feel small. And the smaller they feel, the bigger and badder they fear they look. I know the feeling. I am freed from the chains of those horrible feelings in much the same way that Steve's characters are. An animal shows up, nuzzles my knee or licks my face, and a little twist of fate—or more often, perspective—occurs and I am free again. Free to love my best friend, and my big brother, and maybe even myself.

Steve's books tell us to get mad, think bad thoughts, play out the dark frustration in our heads or with our words, and to then have faith, keep our eyes open, pet a cat, and be willing to receive it if divine grace or human kindness intervenes on our behalf.

I mentioned I also feel too big. I do. My thoughts are big, and my feelings are bigger. My feelings are so big sometimes that I have to do an impression of someone with normal-sized feelings, whatever those are.

Helen Hunt as a child, drawn by Steven Kellogg

Then I read Pinkerton's story, or the Mysterious Tadpole's. They are just too big—for the window, for the leash, for the high school swimming pool. They crash into things right and left. But they don't get knocked down to size at the end of Steve's books; they don't even become better behaved. They, and the people who love them, just find a way to adjust to how big they look on the outside, and how small and vulnerable they feel on the inside.

While I looked through the books in this treasury again, I tried to find the one picture that most feels like Steve to me—a fool's errand, I was sure. And yet . . .

Look at the last picture in *The Christmas Witch.*

Gloria—tiny little witch, smile too big, heart too big, dress *way* too big for her tiny little frame—has the courage to wish for an adventure, and she gets one, and in the process she not only brings peace to a world locked in an unwinnable war, but she creates a new planet. Inclusive, loving, shining out brightly.

This is how I see Steve: heart so big the page won't hold it, giving voice and bringing humor to the mischievous and diabolical in all of us, unwilling to leave any child or librarian behind, uncompromising in his vision of a world that spends money on children and is committed to peace, and above all else, shining out, bright enough to light the whole planet of Pepperdoon . . . with love.

Helen Hunt, 2004

Pinkerton & Friends

Can I Keep Him?

• 1971 •

"Mom, I found this dog sitting all by himself. Can I keep him?"

"No, Arnold. Dogs are too noisy. He would bark all the time and annoy Mr. and Mrs. Van Doon next door. Take him back where you found him."

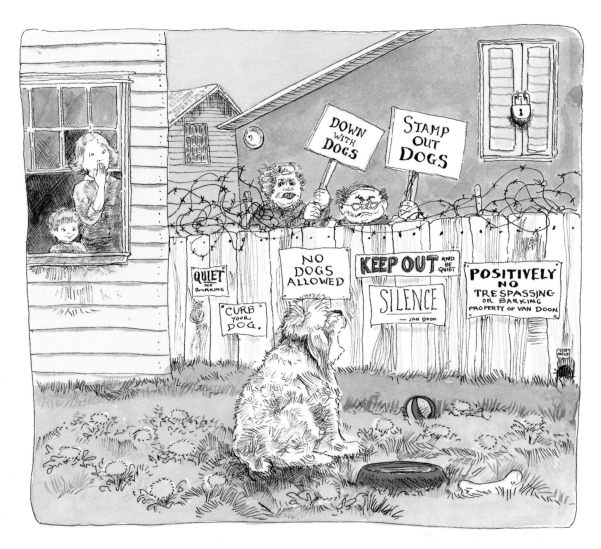

"I found a lost kitten wandering in the street. Can I keep him?"

"No, Arnold. Your grandma is allergic to cat fur. If we kept it, she couldn't visit anymore. Take him back where you found him, and please don't bring any more cats and dogs into the house."

"I found a shy fawn at the edge of the forest. He can't bark, and he doesn't have cat fur. Can I keep him?"

"No, dear. Fawns grow up to be wild bucks. They have sharp hoofs and antlers. In one week our rugs and furniture would be cut to bits."

"A funny little bear fell off a circus train. He wasn't hurt, and I brought him home. He can't bark, he has bear fur, and he has no hoofs. Can I keep him?"

"No, dear. Bears have a disagreeable odor. The house will smell like a circus train."

HOG
PIGEON
Roach-backed
Yugoslavian
Flea-Pecker
(VERY RARE)
flea
?
ZOO

"At the zoo Sweet Sally had three cubs. The zoo keeper said that the zoo only needs two more tigers, so he gave me one for a pet. He can't bark, he has tiger fur, his paws are soft, and he smells nice. Can I keep him?"

"No, dear. Tigers grow up to have terrible appetites. They eat enormous amounts of food, and sometimes they eat people. We could never afford to feed a tiger."

THE FLYING FINKS
80 lbs.
1,237½
13 tons
402 lbs.

WIN
1ST: A DELUXE SURPRISE PRIZE
2ND: A free trip to the MOON
3RD: six fat grape fruits
4TH: a raisin
GUESS THIS PYTHON'S WEIGHT
AND
WIN
THE MYSTERY PRIZE

"A snake man at the carnival ran a contest to see who could guess how much the python weighs. I guessed right, and first prize was the snake. He makes no noise, he has no fur, he has no hoofs, he smells sweet, and he can go for a month without food. Can I keep him?"

“No, dear. Pythons are untidy reptiles. They slither around and shed their scaly skins all over the house. The skins clog the vacuum cleaner.”

DR. KOOT

"In Alaska I saw a scientist chipping a dinosaur out of the ice. When the dinosaur defrosted, he was still alive. The museum didn't want a live dinosaur, so I brought him home. He doesn't bark, he has no fur, he has big soft feet, he doesn't shed—"

"Alaska? When were you ever in Alaska? And who ever heard of a dinosaur for a pet?"

"But I'm lonely. Will you play with me?"

"I'd like to, Arnold, but I'm busy. Why don't you run outside and play on the swing, or ride your bike, or dig in the sandbox?"

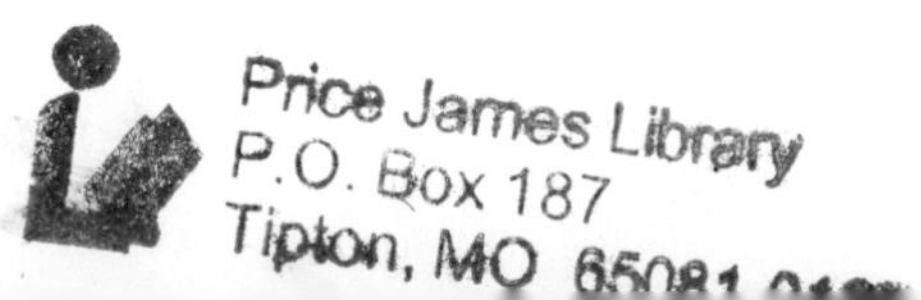

"He just moved in down the street. He doesn't bark, he has no fur, he has no hoofs, he smells like us, he doesn't eat much, he doesn't shed, his name is Ralph, and he says he'll be my friend. Can I keep him?"

“No, dear, you can’t keep him. But he may be your friend and stay and play this afternoon. Now, go outside, and, please, no more questions about ANIMALS!”

Won't Somebody Play with Me?

• 1972 •

"Happy birthday, Kim!"

"When do we open the presents?"

"At five-thirty, when your daddy comes home from work."

"While I'm waiting for five-thirty,
I think I'll go down the hall to Timmy's apartment."

We can play witch and giant or famous generals or maybe we

can pretend that we have an orphanage for lost baby animals.

"Hello, Mrs. Lewis. Can Timmy come out?"

"I'm sorry, Kim, but Timmy has things to do inside for a while. He'll telephone you later when he's finished."

I have to have somebody to play with.
I'll see if my friend Annie is home.

We can play superwomen or doctors or maybe we can run a famous

restaurant and serve pineapple pancakes with bubblegum sauce.

"Hello, Mrs. Schwartz. Can Annie come out?"

"I'm sorry, Kim, but Annie isn't here right now.
She's gone to Timmy's house for the day."

Timmy and Annie! They're probably over there playing witch and giant together!

I'll go to Philip's house.

We can play ape family or spies or maybe we can pretend

that we're fierce, fat dinosaurs munching on bones.

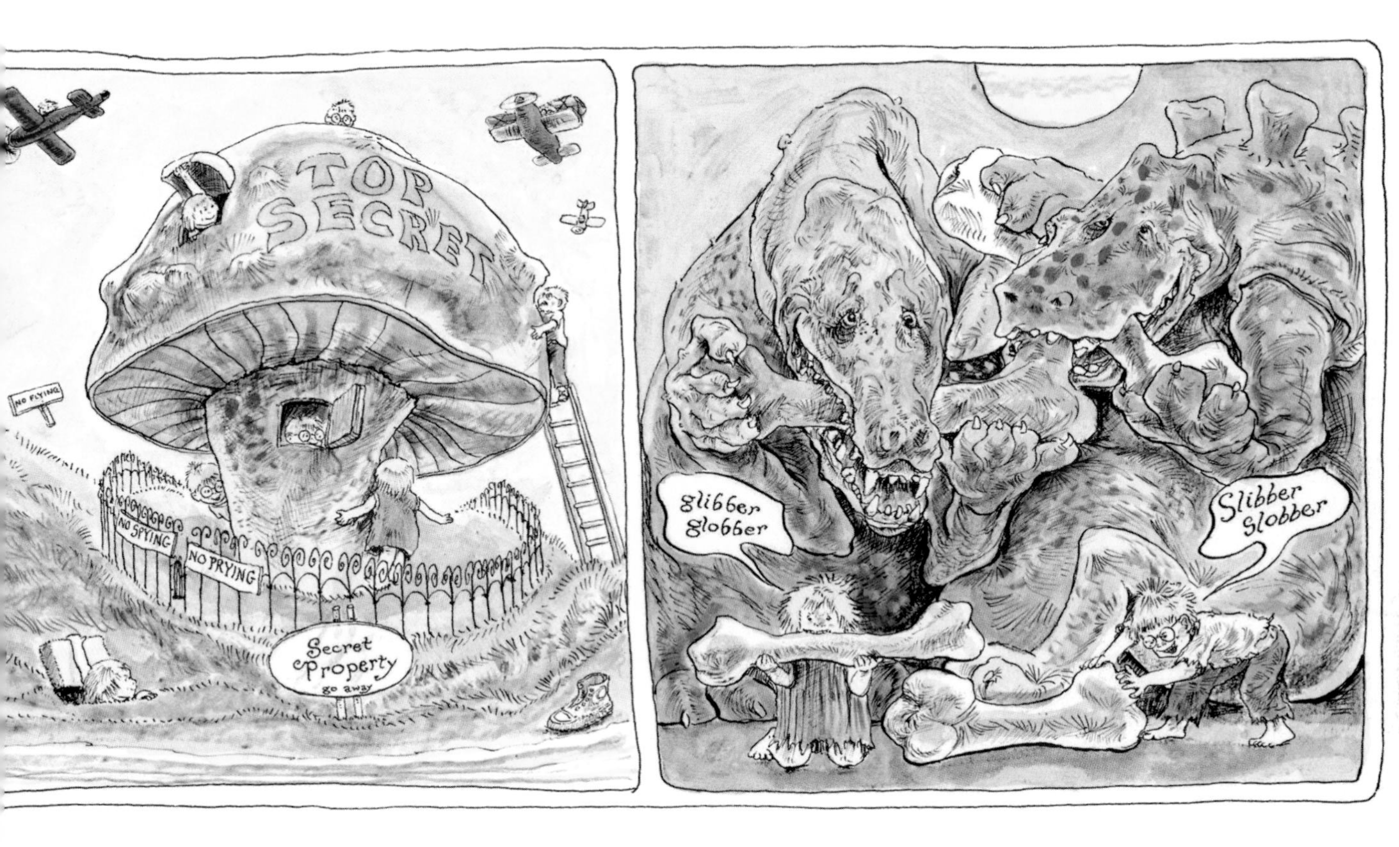

"Hello, Mrs. Orfiello. Can Philip come out?"

"I'm sorry, Kim, but Philip isn't here right now.
He's gone to Timmy's house for the day."

Timmy and Annie and Philip! They're over there together!
I bet they're playing ape family. And there's no one to play with me.

Well, if I were a queen sitting at a huge table piled with desserts, and Timmy and Annie and Philip knocked on the door, I wouldn't let them in! I'd just sit there and stuff myself!

A CHOCOLATE SUNDAE
QUEEN KIM Loves QUEEN KIM
HAPPY DAY TO DEAR ME
TONIGHT
QUEEN KIM
WILL GIVE
A
GRAND
PARTY
no one
is invited
except
The QUEEN And her
Teddy
Give me your
Please can't we play?

If I owned a toy store filled with the best toys in the world, and Timmy and Annie and Philip knocked on the door, I wouldn't let them in. I'd just play and play and play by MYSELF!

LARGER PLAYHOUSES MAY BE ORDERED
CASTLES
CATHEDRALS AND AMPHITHEATERS
MANSIONS & CHATEAUX
PLAYHOUSES
BICYCLES
GOOD BOOKS
Games
BEACH TOYS
NO
CUCKOO HOUSE
TOUR THE SHOP ON OUR MAGIC ROLLER COASTER THEN: ORDER ONE FOR YOUR ROOM
YIPPEE! its on SALE
A GENUINE COVERED WAGON
Buy now and a friendly team of oxen is included at the Bargain Price

If I had a rocket,
and Timmy and Annie
and Philip called on
a walkie-talkie and said,
Can we come too?
I'd yell:
BLAST OFF!

And there I'd be . . .

all by myself . . .

alone.

But, boy, am I mad at Timmy!

And I'm really

mad at Annie!

That stupid Philip!

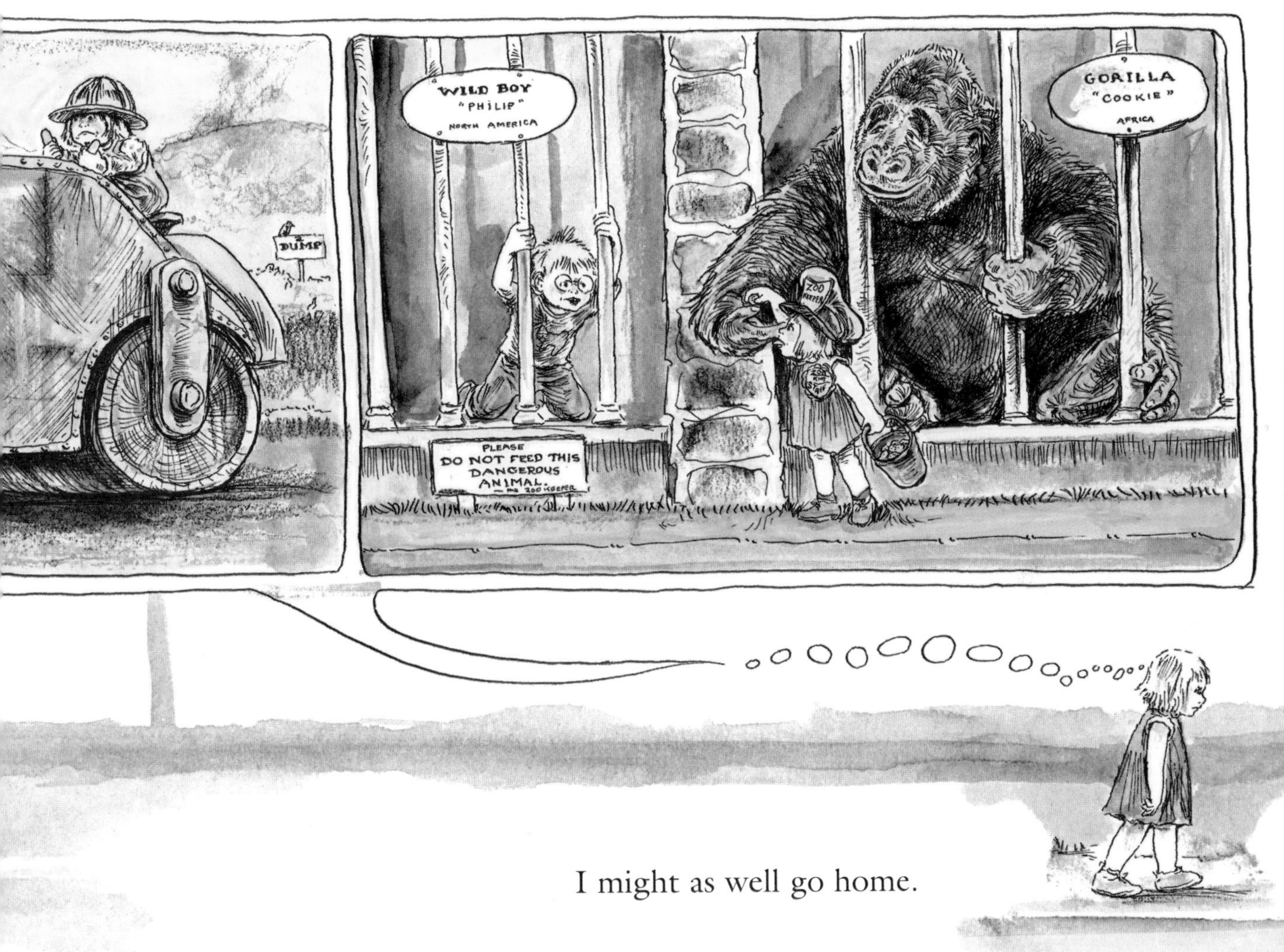

I might as well go home.

"Hello, Kim! How are you?"

"MAD!"

"Would you borrow a cup of sugar for me from Mrs. Lewis?"

"Do I have to?"

"Well, it's for your birthday cake."
"Okay."
21a

"Hello, Kim. We were just about to call you."

SURPRISE!

HAPPY BIRTHDAY
KIM the GREAT
HAPPY BIRTHDAY
To ANNIE'S PAL
KIM
LOVE FROM YOUR FRIEND ANNIE

The Island of the Skog

• 1973 •

NATIONAL
RODENT
DAY
An Antique
clock case.

It was National Rodent Day, and Jenny decided to have a party. Hannah, Wooster, and Louise came. So did Bouncer and his buddies from the bowling alley.

They all arrived shaking after a narrow escape from the butcher's cat. Jenny decided to wheel in the dessert right away.

"Hot marshmallow cheesecake with raspberry fudge sauce!" she announced.

Meanwhile the cat had slipped in with the delivery boy. The mice just barely escaped to the basement.

“A German shepherd got Granny last night,” puffed Hannah. “We should stay in our own holes!”

“I’m tired of living in a hole,” said Jenny.

“Let’s fight for freedom!” cried Bouncer. “We’ll be soldiers! Rough-riding Rowdies! I’ll be the general and commander in chief!”

“Wait!” cried Jenny. “Let’s sail away instead. We’ll find a peaceful island.”

The mice cheered.

“I’ll be the ship’s captain!” declared Bouncer. “Rowdies, you’re my crew!”

It took the mice most of the night to load the ship and roll it to the harbor.

Ignoring the crowd at the pier, they sailed bravely out to sea.

During the first few days of the voyage the mice feasted on chocolate waffles and coconut cherry cheese pie. Between meals they dreamed of their island and tanned their pelts in the sun.

THE ROWDIES
RODENT LEAGUE
BOWLING
CHAMPS
1973
1967
1963
IN PURSUIT OF HAPPINESS
TRUTH
JUSTICE
EQUALITY
LIBERTY
BROTHERHOOD
PEACE & LOVE
TWELVE
CANNONBALLS
FOR
CANNONS
GEOGRAPHY

As the days passed, it grew colder and colder. The mice were unprepared for winter weather, and they huddled close to the waffle iron.

"Land ho!" cried Captain Bouncer one morning as the ship narrowly missed hitting an iceberg. The mice looked at the compass and discovered that they had been sailing toward the North Pole.

"The compass must've been upside down!" insisted Bouncer. "I'm tired of being captain anyway. I quit!"

By the time they reached warmer seas, their food supplies were very low. The mice were seasick, homesick, and convinced they would soon be dead.

"I'd give a billion dollars for one last chocolate-coated cheese puff," moaned a Rowdy.

Suddenly Jenny cried: "Land ho!"

"The book calls it the Island of the Skog," said Wooster. "It says: 'Population: One Skog.' But it doesn't say what a Skog is."

"If there's only one, then there's plenty of room for all of us," said Louise. "Why don't we bring it a gift so it will know we're friendly?"

"Wait a minute, flubberhead," snapped Bouncer. "Suppose this Skog is dangerous? Let's blaze our way to the island and show him we mean business!"

The Rowdies fired all twelve cannonballs, and then the mice waded cautiously ashore.

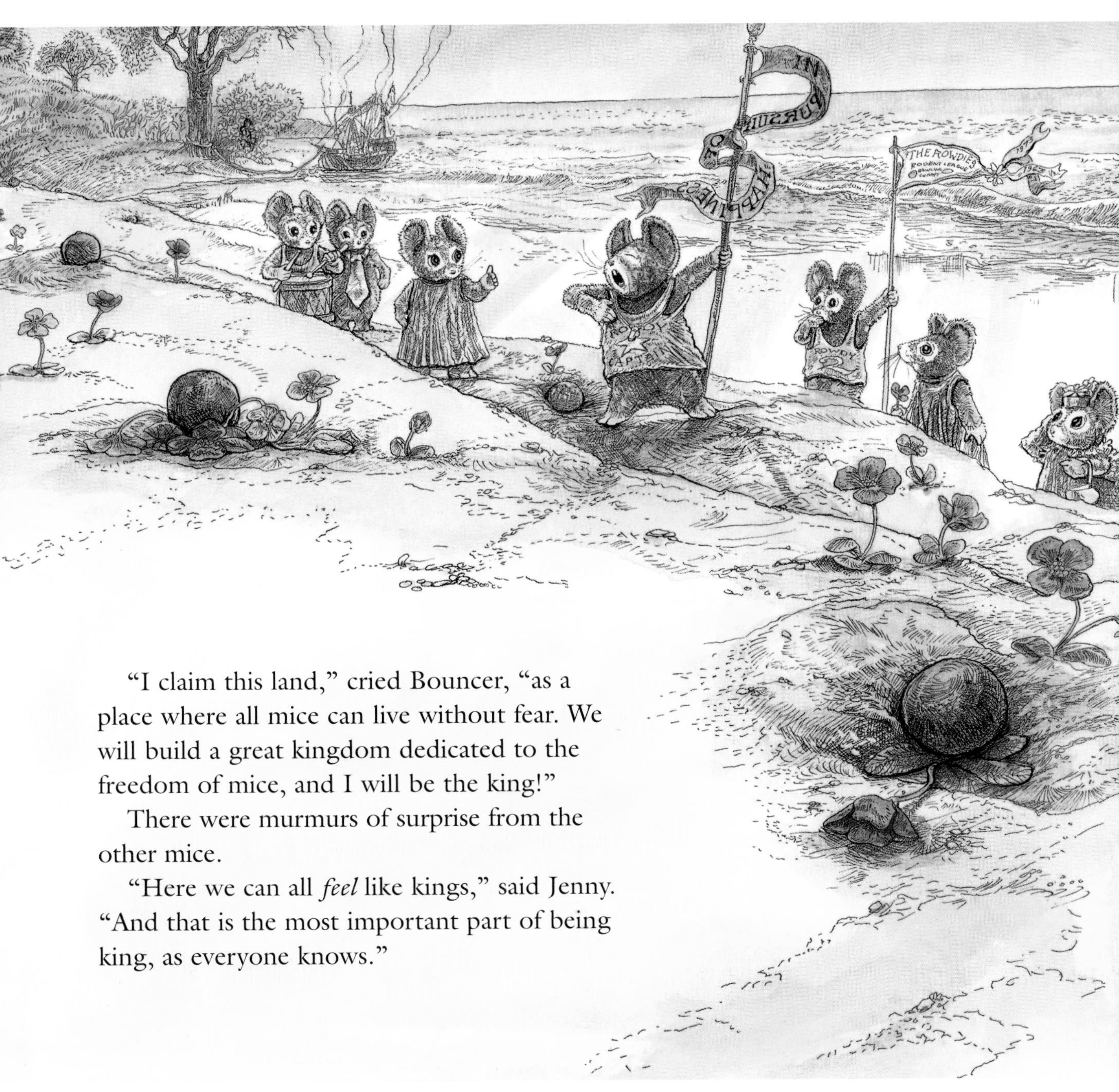

"I claim this land," cried Bouncer, "as a place where all mice can live without fear. We will build a great kingdom dedicated to the freedom of mice, and I will be the king!"

There were murmurs of surprise from the other mice.

"Here we can all *feel* like kings," said Jenny. "And that is the most important part of being king, as everyone knows."

After unloading their supplies, they somersaulted on the beach through the long, brilliant sunset. How wonderful it was to be on land again.

Finally, as the last rays of daylight faded, they climbed back aboard the ship to spend the night.

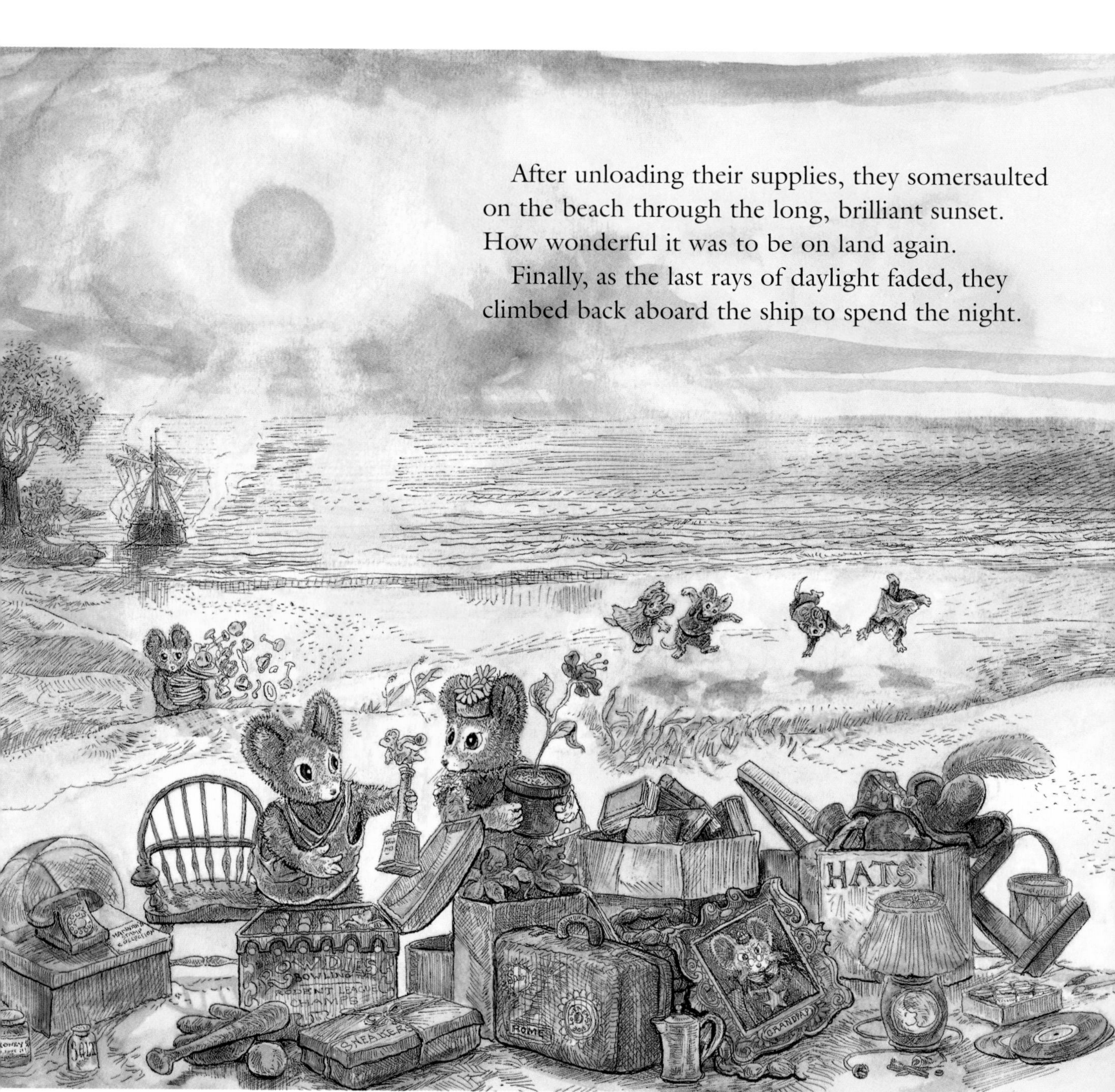

At dawn, they discovered an enormous footprint in the sand.

"It looks like a bear track," said Hannah.

"Stand aside, tenderfeet," ordered Bouncer. "This is a job for the Rough-riding Rowdies! We'll use my granpap's favorite trick. First dig a deep hole, then cover it with straw, and bait it with honey. Tonight the beast will smell the bait, stumble into the trap, and the island will be ours!"

By evening the trap was completed. The mice spent a sleepless night in a nearby hole.

The next morning they discovered that the trap was empty. "Look!" shrieked Hannah. "Someone cut the rope. The ship is gone."

"We're MAROONED!" wailed the mice.

"Our only chance now," said Bouncer, "is to get rid of the Skog before he gets rid of us. Who will volunteer?"

"It looks like a job for the Rough-riding Rowdies," said Jenny.

"Whose idea was it to come here anyway?" grumbled Bouncer.

All eyes turned back to Jenny.

"I have a plan," she said. "We must build a giant kite and tie it to a very long rope. We'll circle a honey jar with one end of the rope, and when the Skog steps into the circle, we will send the kite aloft. The Skog will be pulled into the air and towed out to sea."

That night the mice hid behind a sand dune and kept watch over the honey jar. Just after dawn a shadowy figure appeared on the beach.

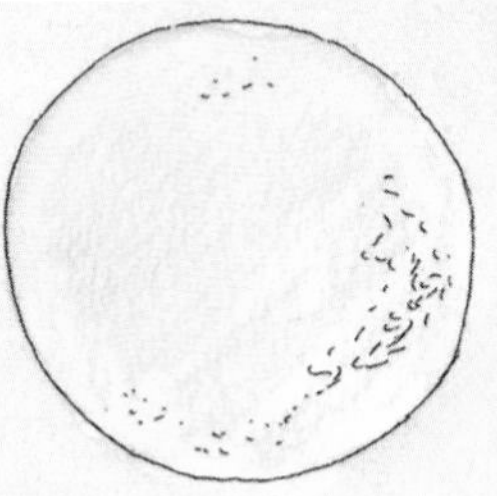

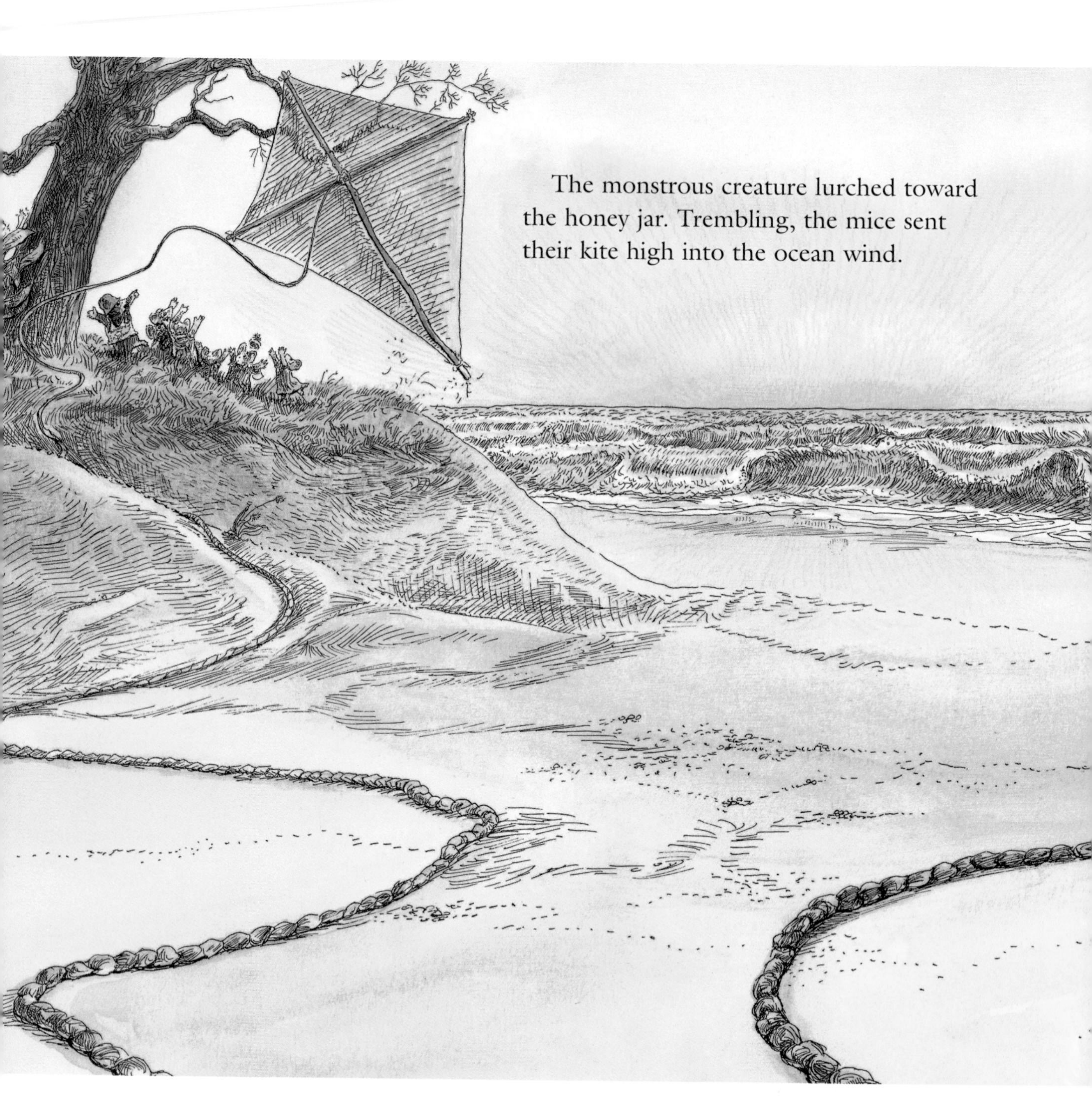

The monstrous creature lurched toward the honey jar. Trembling, the mice sent their kite high into the ocean wind.

HONEY
YOU'LL LOVE IT!

The plan had worked! But suddenly the Skog came flapping apart, and half of him plunged back to the island.

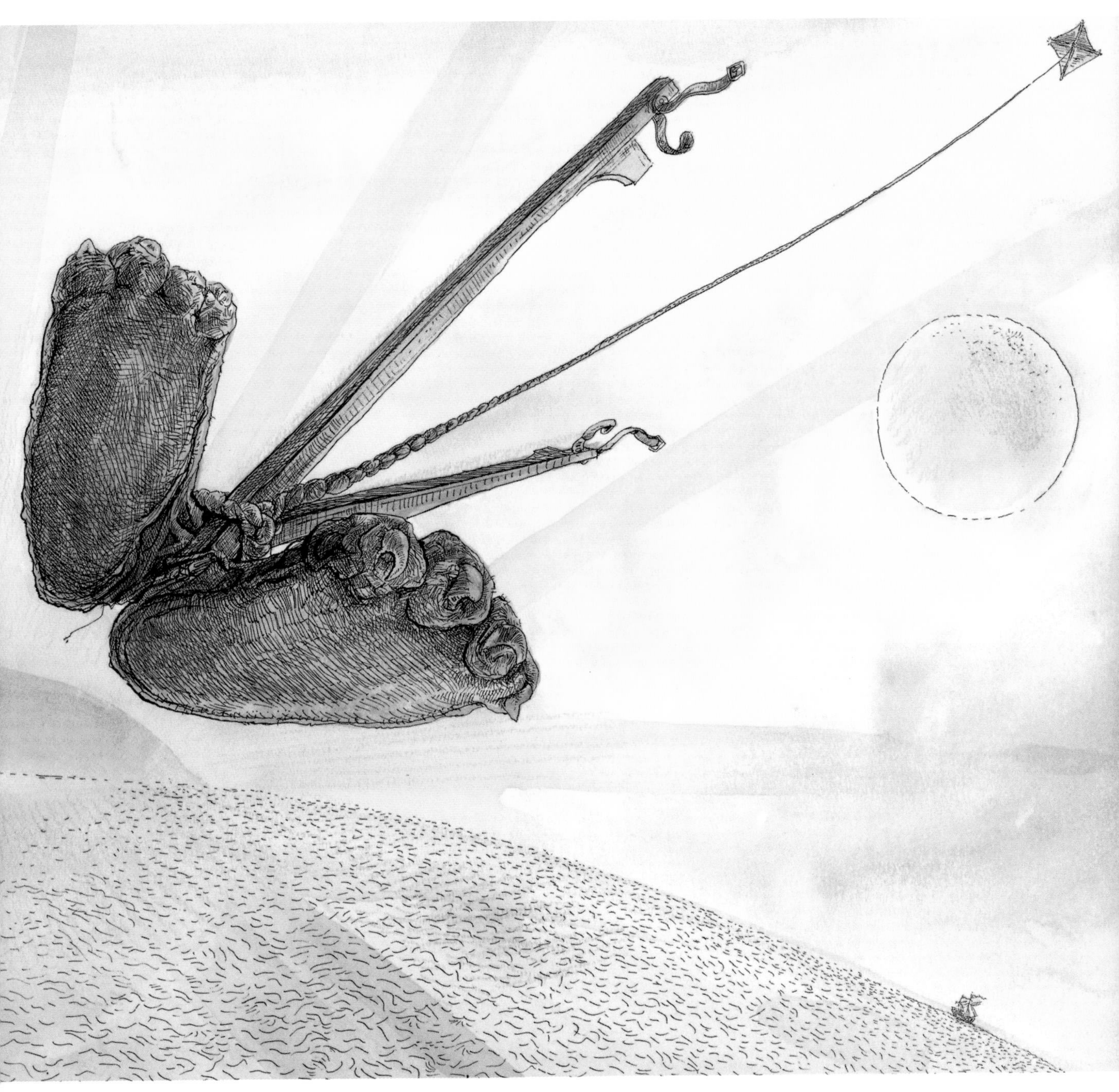

The fallen Skog lay flat and still.

"Surrender, you pirate!" puffed Bouncer.

Suddenly a little animal appeared. "Don't hurt me!" he cried.

"We won't hurt you," said Wooster. "We were afraid of you! Why did you wear this monster costume?"

"Because I was afraid of you!" cried the Skog. "I was frightened by your cannons and your trap!"

“What happened to our ship?” demanded Bouncer.

“I cut the rope because I thought you were sleeping on board,” confessed the Skog. “I’ve been so lonely here, but I decided it was better to be alone than to be afraid.”

“If only we’d talked to each other,” said Jenny.

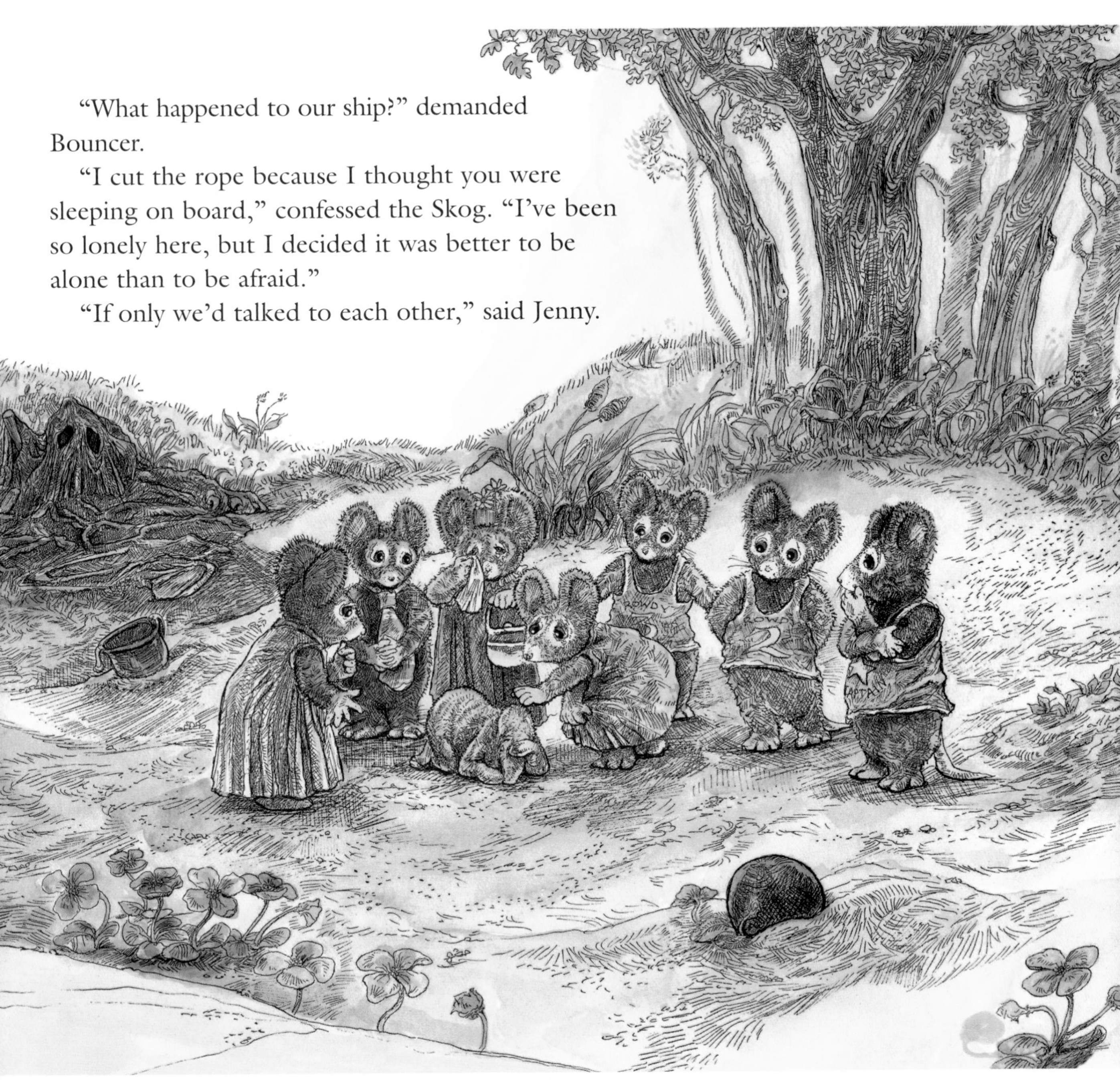

Bouncer stepped forward and helped the Skog to his feet.

They all agreed to build a village and live together.

"Let's make plans right now!" suggested Bouncer. "The first thing we'll need is a national anthem. Rowdies, you're the orchestra. The rest of you will be the chorus, and I will lead the music. Line up, everybody!"

Heroes, let your voices ring.
To our island home we sing.
Shelter us from stormy seas.
Keep our kitchens stuffed with cheese.
Save our pelts from lice and fleas.
Save our pelts from fleas and lice.
Shout it once! Shout it twice!
Friends forever! Skog and mice!

Much Bigger Than Martin

• 1976 •

Sometimes it's fun being Martin's little brother.

But I hate it when he says, "Let's form a line. The biggest is first. The smallest is last."

Then he makes me play his stupid games.

THE CHIEF

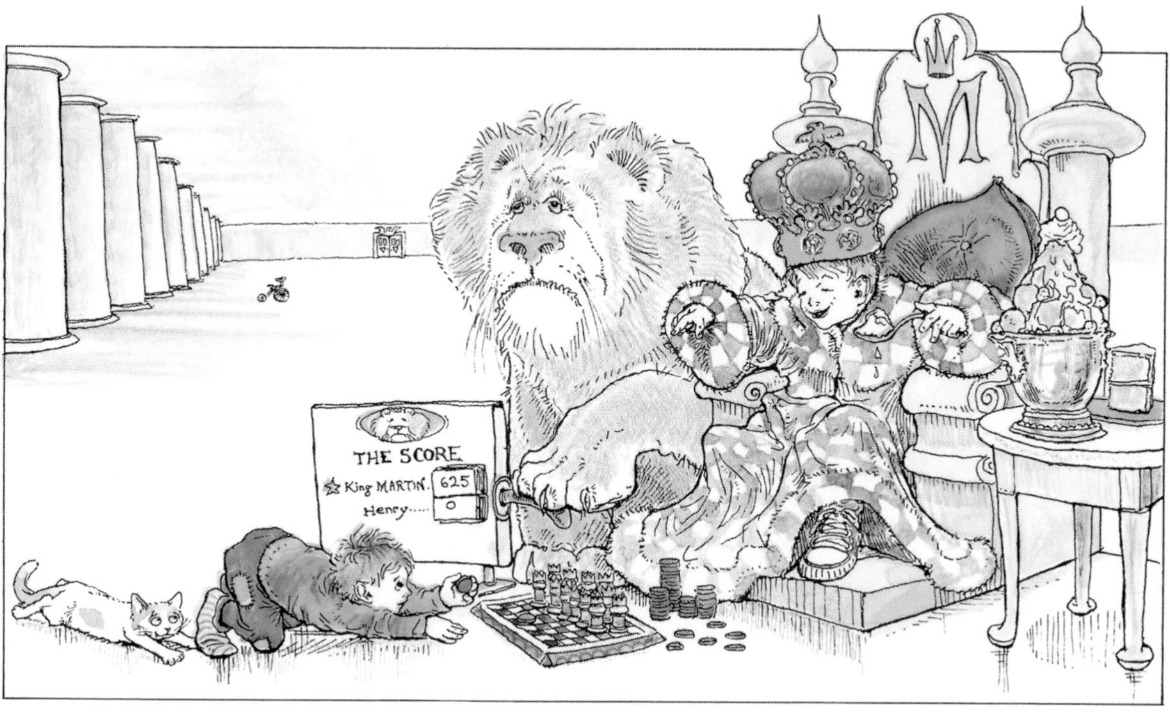
M
THE SCORE
King MARTIN 625
Henry..... 0

When we go to the beach with his friends, he says, "You're too small to swim to the raft."

And when he cuts the cake for our dessert, he says, "The biggest person gets the biggest piece."

Once when his friends were there, I was playing basketball. Martin said, "Better luck next year, shorty." All those big kids laughed.

I wished that I could grow bigger than Martin.

Much bigger!

I tried to stretch myself.

Then I tried watering myself.

Then I remembered that Grandpa said, "Apples make you grow!"

I told Martin my plan. He said I'd grow into a giant apple.

He said he'd put me in a circus and become famous.

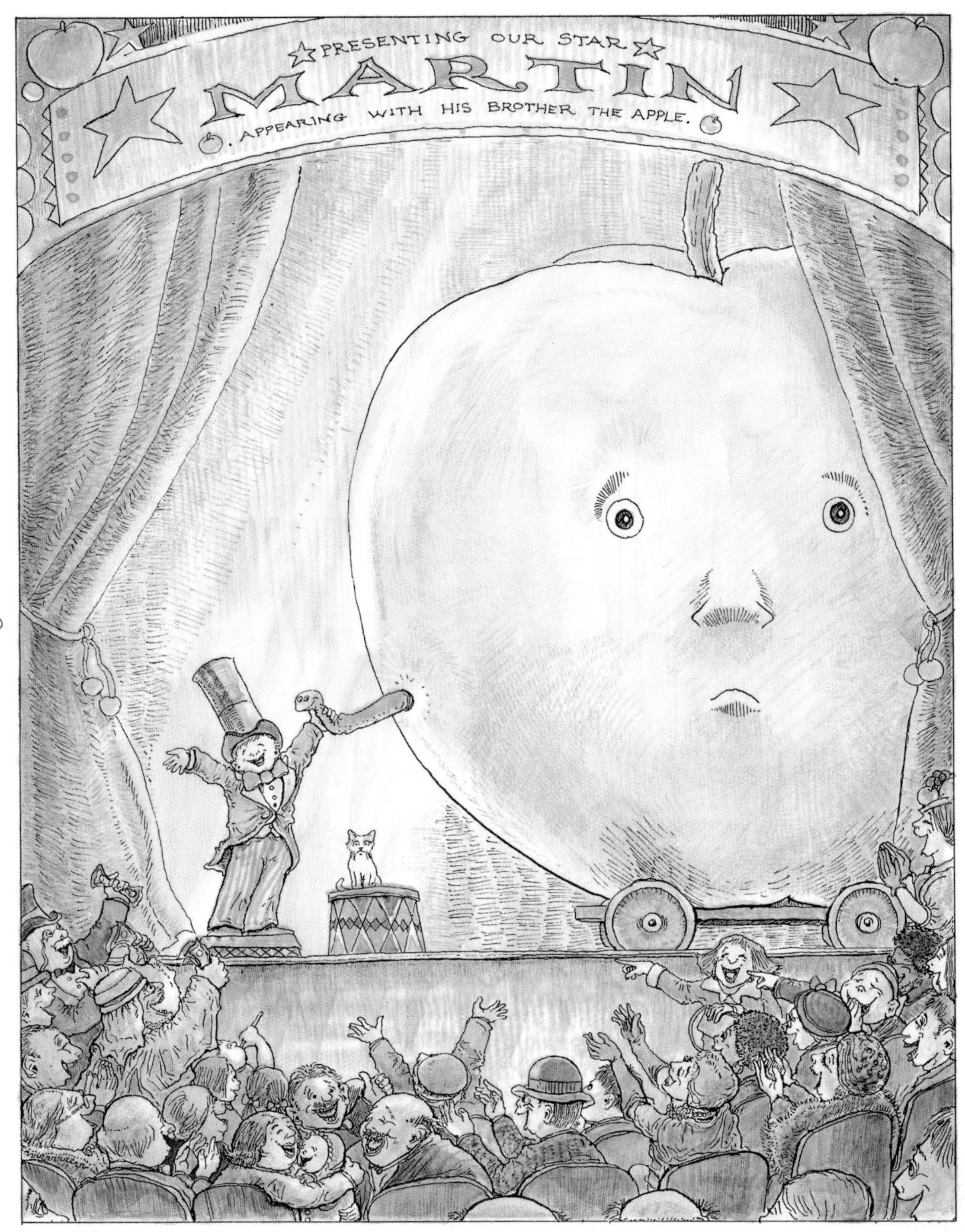

"You'll be sorry, Martin," I said.

"When I'm a giant, I'll grind your bones to make my bread."

RYE
RAISIN
UNTOASTED
TOASTED
BURNED
CRUST
NO CRUST
ALL CRUST
FRESH
STALE
THE BONE GRINDER
THE SLICER
ON
NOT ON
POACH
SCRAMBLE
MASH
CRUMBS

I ate every apple, but I didn't grow at all.

I just felt sick.

When Martin screamed, *"Dinnertime!"* I said, "Get out or you'll get bitten by a sick giant."

Mom heard me groaning. She said, "Why did you eat all those apples?"

"So I could grow bigger than Martin," I told her. "*Much* bigger! As big as a *giant*!"

Dad said, "Why do you want to be bigger than Martin?"

"So I can go to the raft with all the kids," I said.

“And divide the cake so that I can get the biggest part and Martin gets one crumb.

And make a basket so easily that Martin and his friends will never laugh."

Mom said, “If you were a giant, you’d be too big to fit in the house.”

"Besides," said Dad, "when Martin was your age, he was just your size. You're wearing his old blue pajamas!"

When Martin came to bed, he said, "Sorry you feel like a rotten apple."

Then he said, "Tomorrow I'll give you a surprise and tell you a secret."

The surprise was a new basket that Martin and Dad put up just for me.

Then Martin told me his secret. He said, “When I was your age, I couldn’t reach that high basket either.”

So Martin and I were friends again.

But the next day he said, "Let's play ape hunt. I'll be the hunter because I'm bigger, and you can be the little ape who gets captured."

I said, "That doesn't sound like much fun. Besides, I'm making something in the garage."

SEE MY
APE
5¢

Pinkerton, Behave!

• 1979 •

Every new puppy has to learn to behave.
First I'll teach Pinkerton to come when he's called.

He can learn to bring us the newspaper.

THE TIMES
ELECTION: WHO? WHY?

Fetch!

GOOD NEWS
STOP
GRRRRRRRRRRRRRRRRRRRRRRRRRRRRRRRRRRRRRRRRRR

From now on *I'll* fetch the newspaper.

But it's important for him to defend the house if a burglar comes.

We'll pretend this dummy is a burglar.

Get the burglar, Pinkerton!

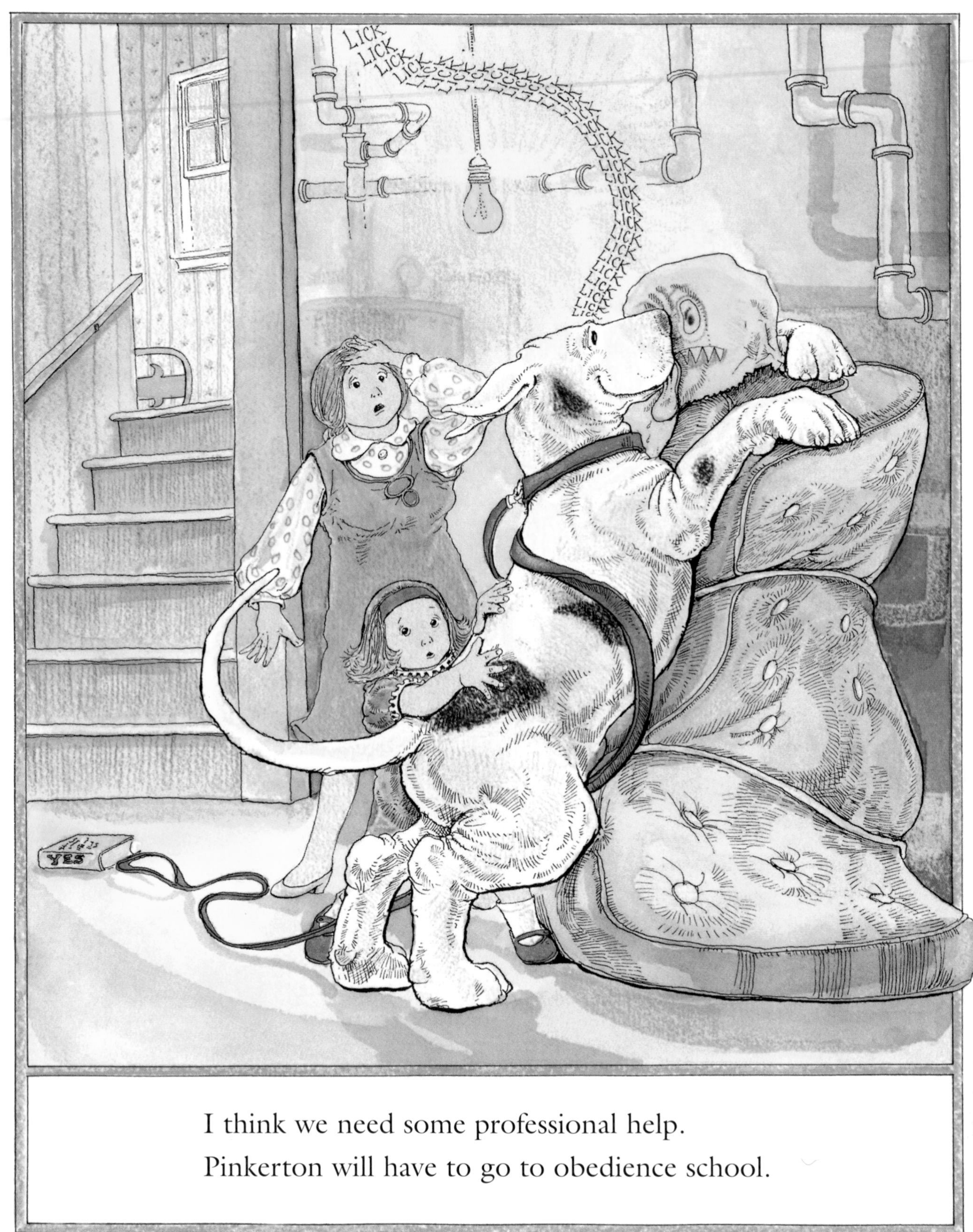

I think we need some professional help.
Pinkerton will have to go to obedience school.

When this poor creature sees how well the other dogs behave, he will understand what we expect of him.

We begin with a simple command. Come.

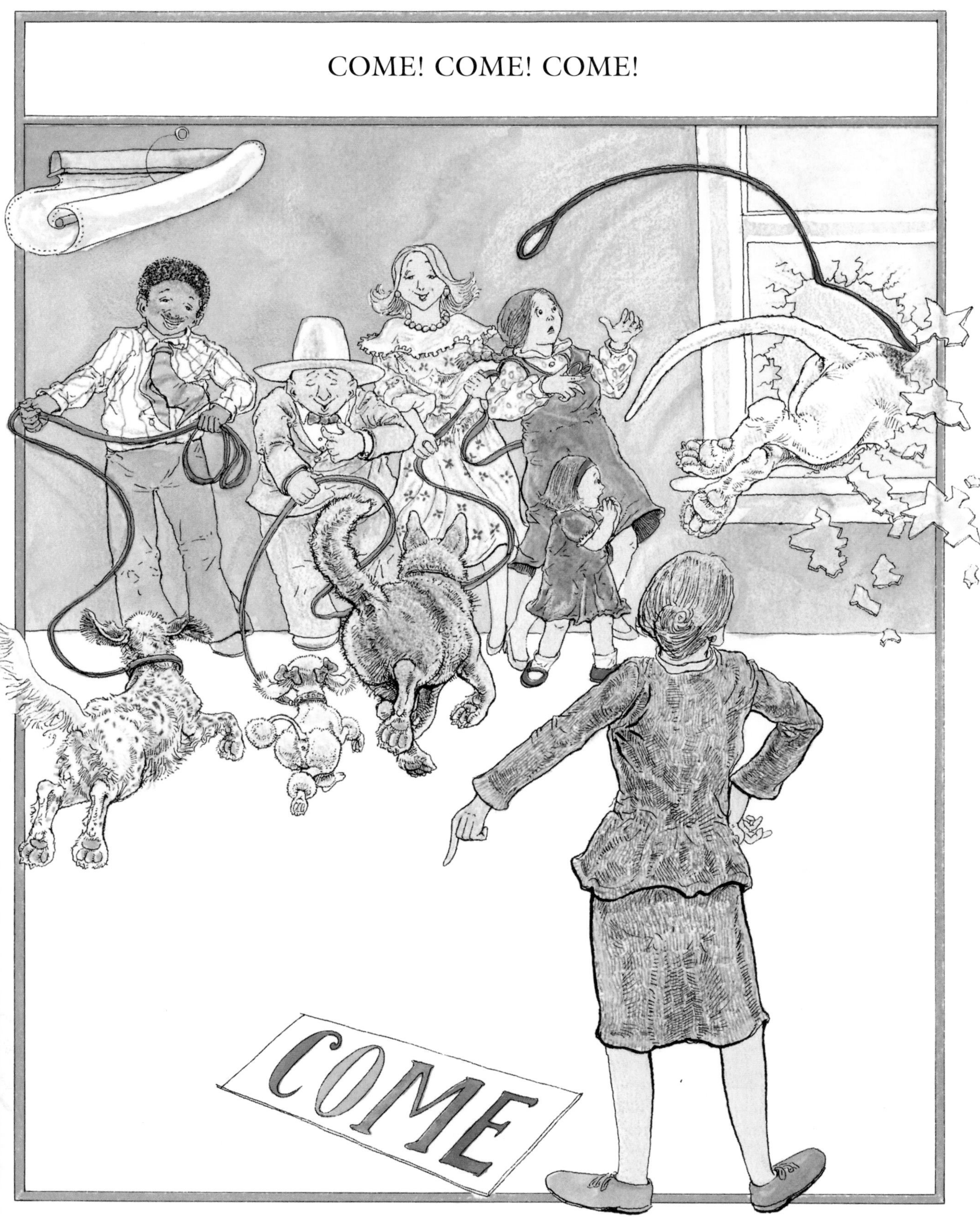
COME! COME! COME!
COME

We cannot hold back the entire class for one confused student. On to the next lesson!

Every dog must fetch the evening paper.

Fetch, you fleabrain, FETCH!

Our next lesson is a most important one.
Get the burglar!

GRRRRRRRRRRRRRRRRrrrrr
BURGLAR
GRRRRRRRRRRRRRRRRRRrrrrr
BURGLAR
GRRRRRRRRRRRRRRRRRrrrrr
BURGLAR
LICK
LICK
LICK
LICK
LICK
LICK
LICK
LICK
LICK
LICK

Pinkerton sets a poor example for the rest of the class. Unless he shows some improvement, he will be dismissed.

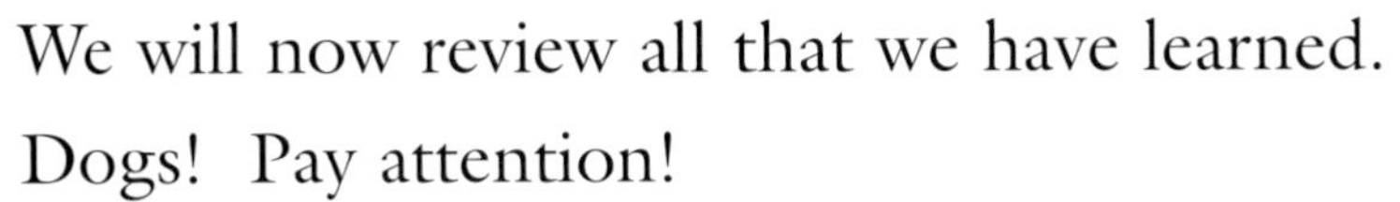

We will now review all that we have learned.
Dogs! Pay attention!

COME!

LICK
LICK
LICK
LICK
LICK
LICK
LICK
LICK
LICK
LICK
LICK
LICK
LICK
FETCH!
TIMES
GRRRRRRRRRRRRRRRRRRRRRRRRRRRRRRRRRR

GET THE BURGLAR!

OUT! OUT! OUT! OUT!

Mom, you and Pinkerton look pretty tired.
Why don't you go to bed and get a good night's rest?

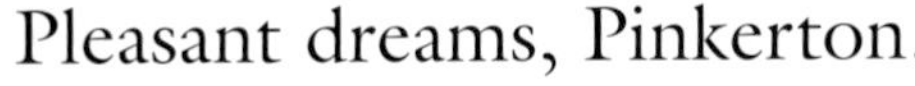

Pleasant dreams, Pinkerton.

FETCH
FETCH
TIME
GRRRRRRRRRRRRRRRR

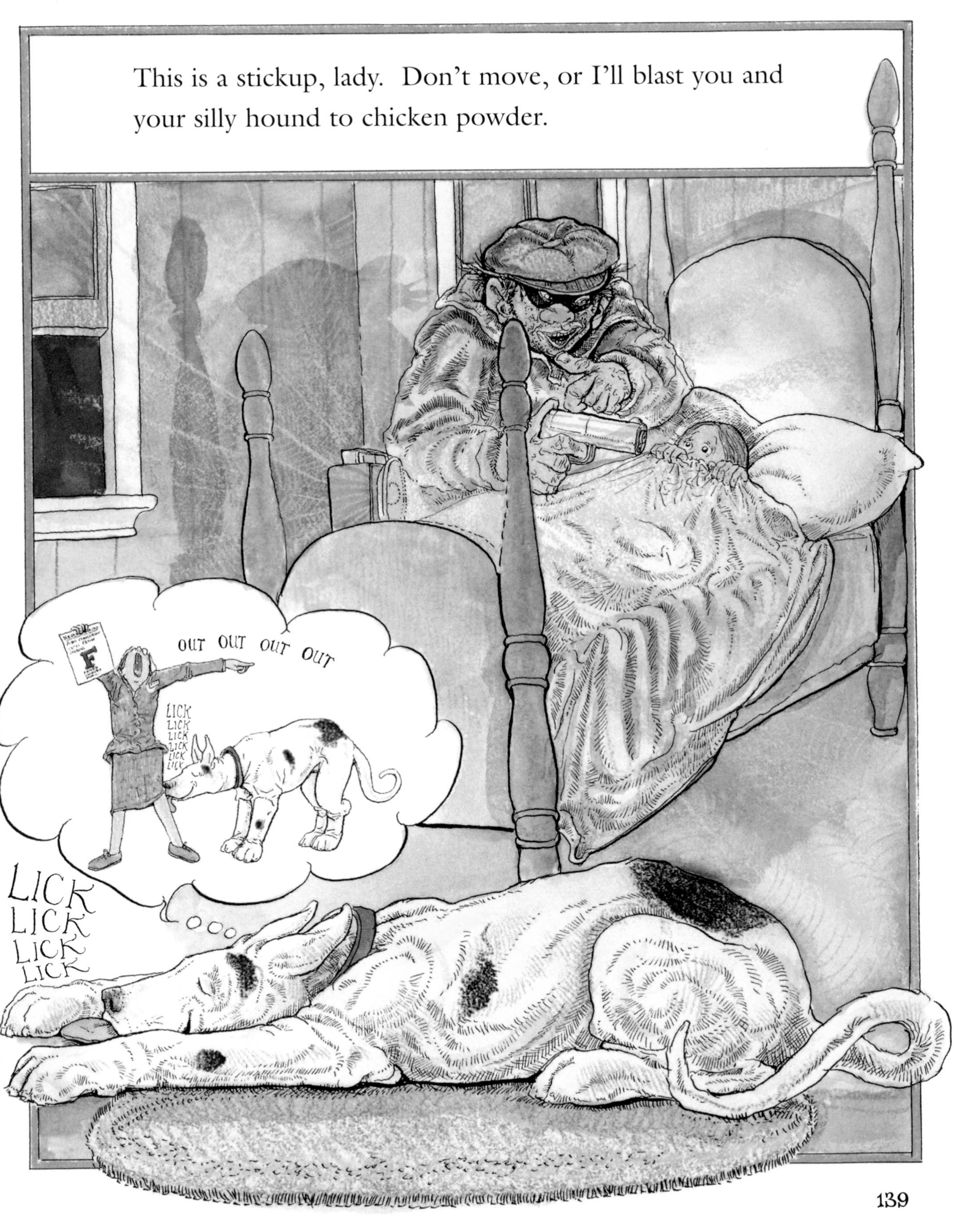
This is a stickup, lady. Don't move, or I'll blast you and your silly hound to chicken powder.
OUT OUT OUT OUT
LICK LICK LICK LICK LICK LICK
LICK LICK LICK LICK

Psssssst! Pinkerton! A burglar!

I warned you, lady.

Pinkerton! Fetch!

GRRRRRRRRRRRRR

Pinkerton! Come!

Pinkerton, I'm a burglar.

I love you, Pinkerton.

The Day Jimmy's Boa Ate the Wash

by Trinka Hakes Noble

• 1980 •

"How was your class trip to the farm?"

"Oh . . . boring . . . kind of dull . . . until the cow started crying."

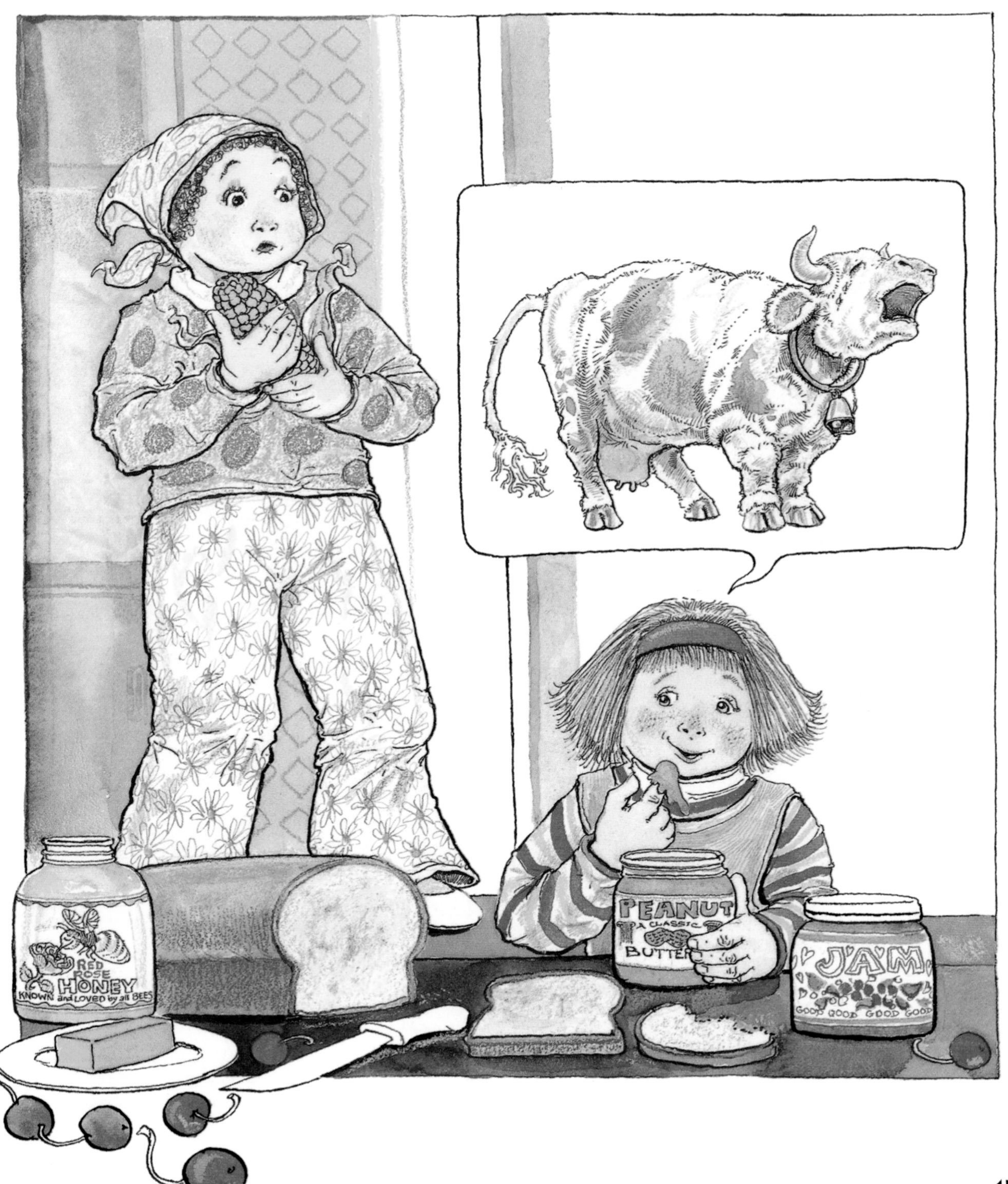

"A cow . . . crying?"
"Yeah, you see, a haystack fell on her."

"But a haystack doesn't just fall over."

“It does if a farmer crashes into it with his tractor.”
“Oh, come on, a farmer wouldn’t do that.”

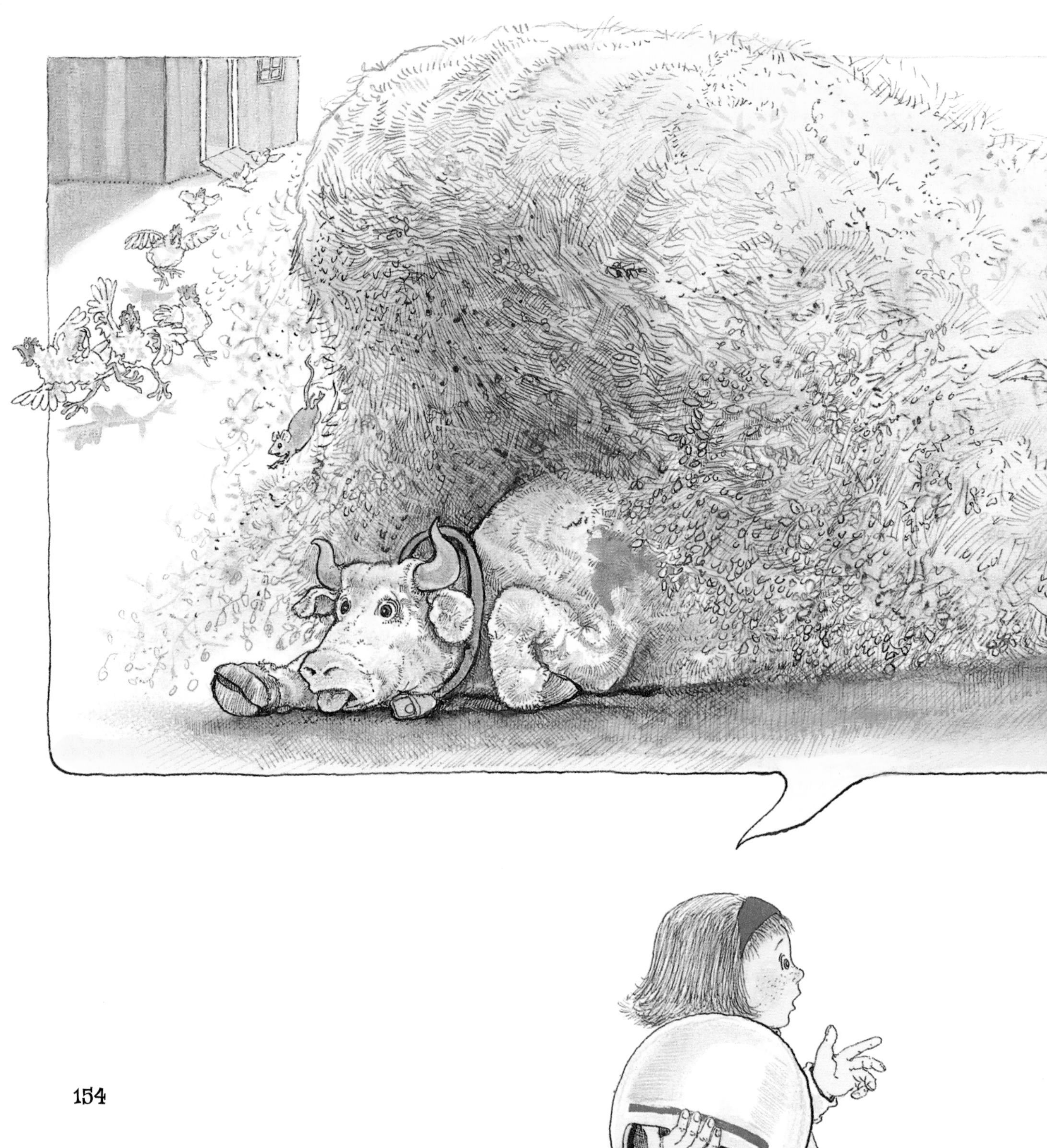

"He would if he were too busy yelling at the pigs to get off our school bus."

"What were the pigs doing on the bus?"

"Eating our lunches."

“Why were they eating your lunches?”
“Because we threw their corn at each other, and they didn’t have anything else to eat.”

"Well, that makes sense, but why were you throwing corn?"
"Because we ran out of eggs."
"Out of eggs? Why were you throwing eggs?"

"Because of the boa constrictor."
"THE BOA CONSTRICTOR!"
"Yeah, Jimmy's pet boa constrictor."

"What was Jimmy's pet boa constrictor doing on the farm?"
"Oh, he brought it to meet all the farm animals,
but the chickens didn't like it."

"You mean he took it into the henhouse?"

"Yeah, and the chickens started squawking and flying around."

"Go on, go on. What happened?"

"Well, one hen got excited and laid an egg, and it landed on Jenny's head."

"The hen?"

"No, the egg. And it broke—yucky—all over her hair."

"What did she do?"
"She got mad because she thought Tommy threw it, so she threw one at him."
"What did Tommy do?"
"Oh, he ducked and the egg hit Marianne in the face.

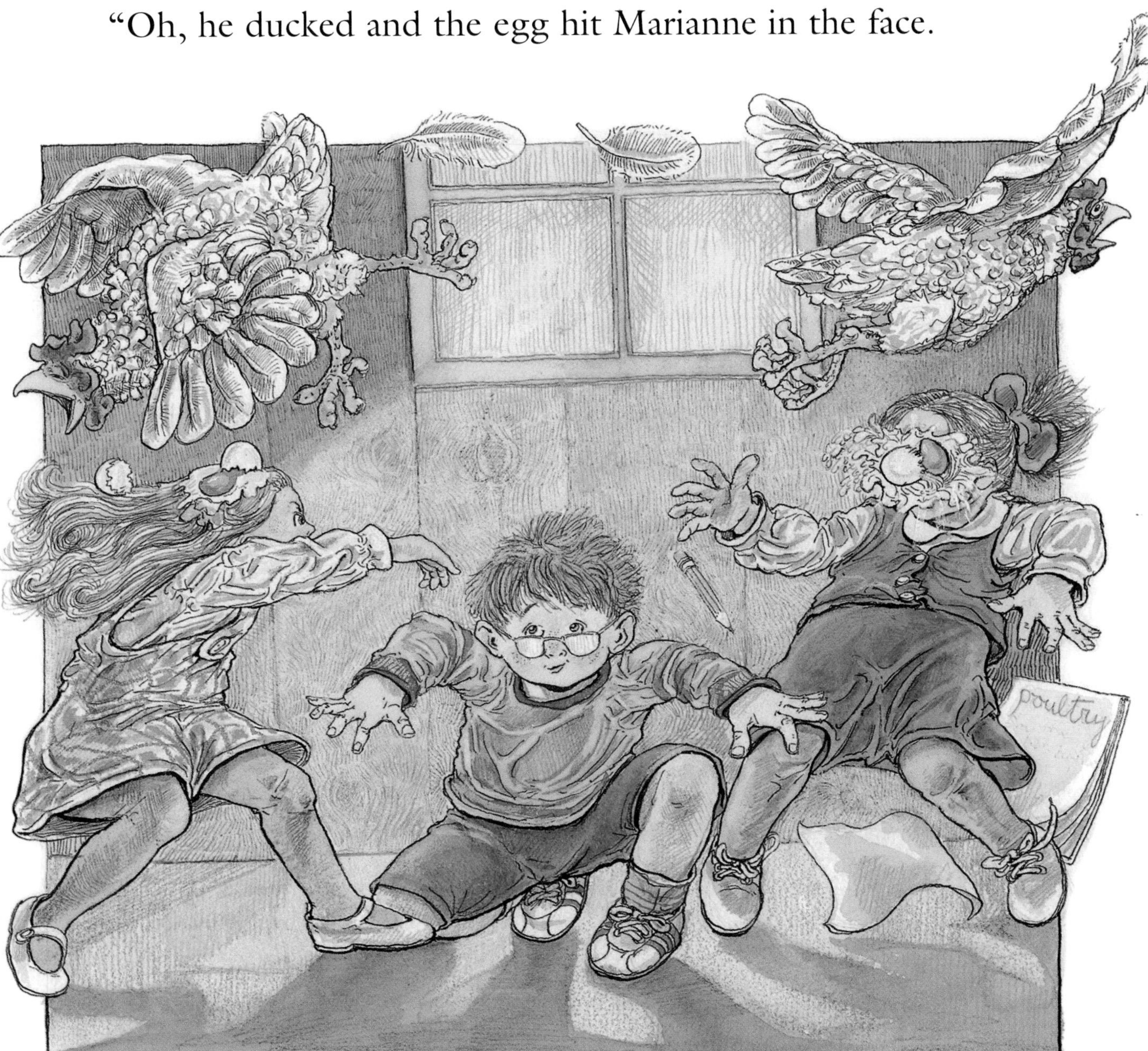

"So she threw one at Jenny, but she missed and hit Jimmy, who dropped his boa constrictor."

“Oh, I know, and the next thing you knew, everyone was throwing eggs, right?”

“Right.”

"And when you ran out of eggs, you threw the pigs' corn, right?"

"Right again."

"Well, what finally stopped it?"
"Well, we heard the farmer's wife screaming."
"Why was she screaming?"

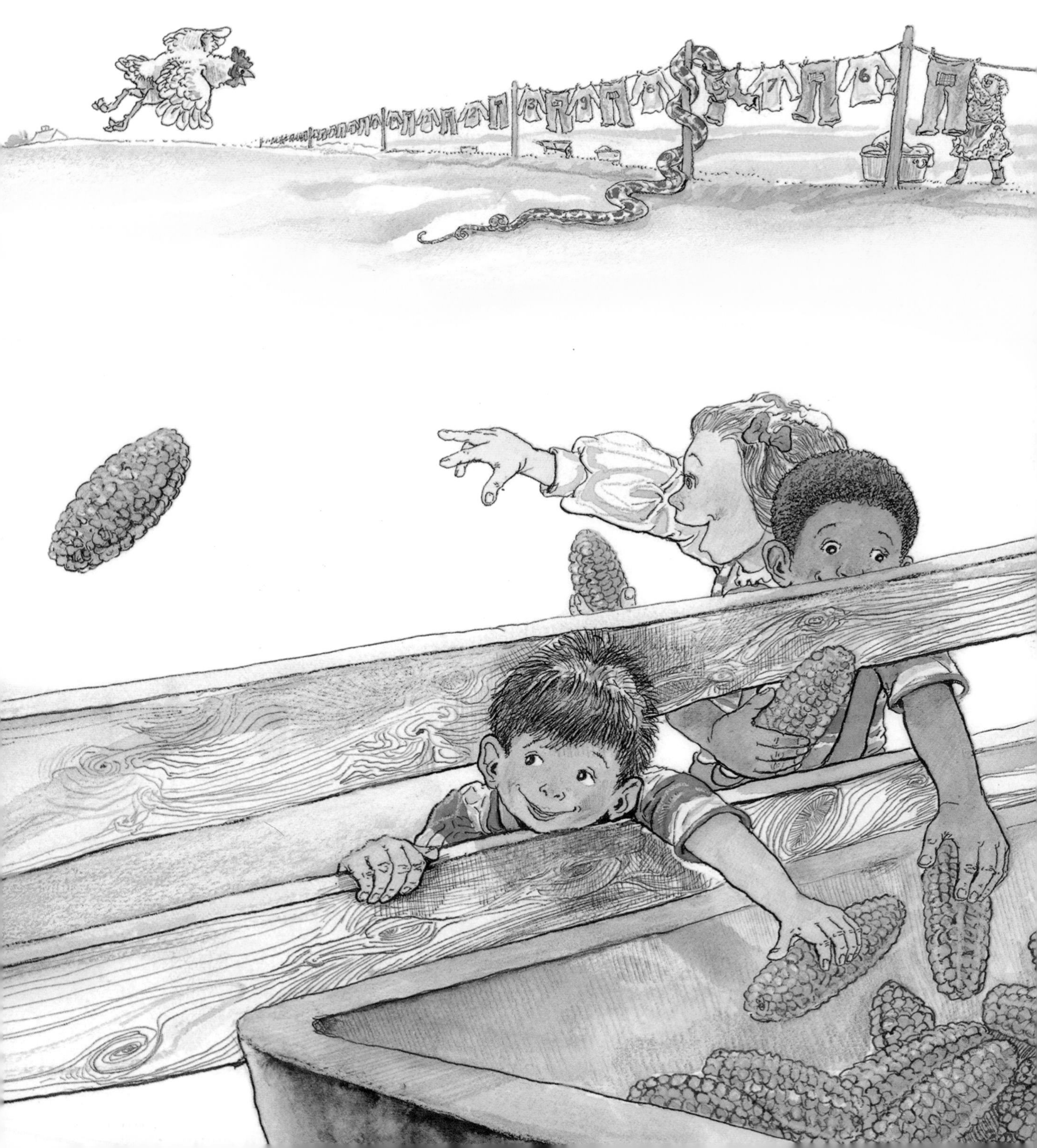

"We never found out, because Mrs. Stanley made us get on the bus, and we sort of left in a hurry without the boa constrictor."

"I bet Jimmy was sad because he left his pet boa constrictor."

"Oh, not really. We left in such a hurry that one of the pigs didn't get off the bus, so now he's got a pet pig."

"Boy, that sure sounds like an exciting trip."

"Yeah, I suppose, if you're the kind of kid who likes class trips to the farm."

GRAND PRIX

OUR
BOA

Ralph's Secret Weapon

• 1983 •

After successfully completing the third grade, Ralph was sent to vacation with his aunt Georgiana. She greeted him with a banana-spinach cream cake and the news that he would spend the summer learning to play the bassoon.

"This cake is from a recipe that I created myself," said Aunt Georgiana proudly. "I believe in keeping busy," she added, "and I hope you will study the bassoon with the same energy that I put into all of my projects."

"I'll try," said Ralph.

Aunt Georgiana's house was like a castle. Ralph wanted to explore it and to play with her Great Danes, but she had already planned his afternoon.

"It's important for you to begin practicing immediately," explained Aunt Georgiana. "Your teacher, the famous Maestro Preposteroso, is coming tonight for your first lesson."

Aunt Georgiana left for the afternoon, and Ralph, feeling the need for a snack, went to find the kitchen.

As he entered, he saw a mouse nibbling his cake. To his surprise it instantly became very sick.

"I better not eat this thing," Ralph decided, and he hid it in the back of his closet.

During Ralph's first bassoon lesson the sour notes he produced brought worms dancing out of apples.

"He is hopeless. I see no talent whatsoever!" cried the maestro.

"Nonsense!" declared Aunt Georgiana. "He shows great promise as a snake charmer! There is an international snake charming competition opening at the colosseum tonight, and Ralph and I will be there!" She dismissed the maestro and called for her car.

They arrived just as the snakes were slithering onto the stage and the snake charmers were tuning their instruments.

"What an exciting event!" declared Aunt Georgiana.

Ralph wasn't sure he wanted to sign up.

"Nonsense!" declared his aunt.

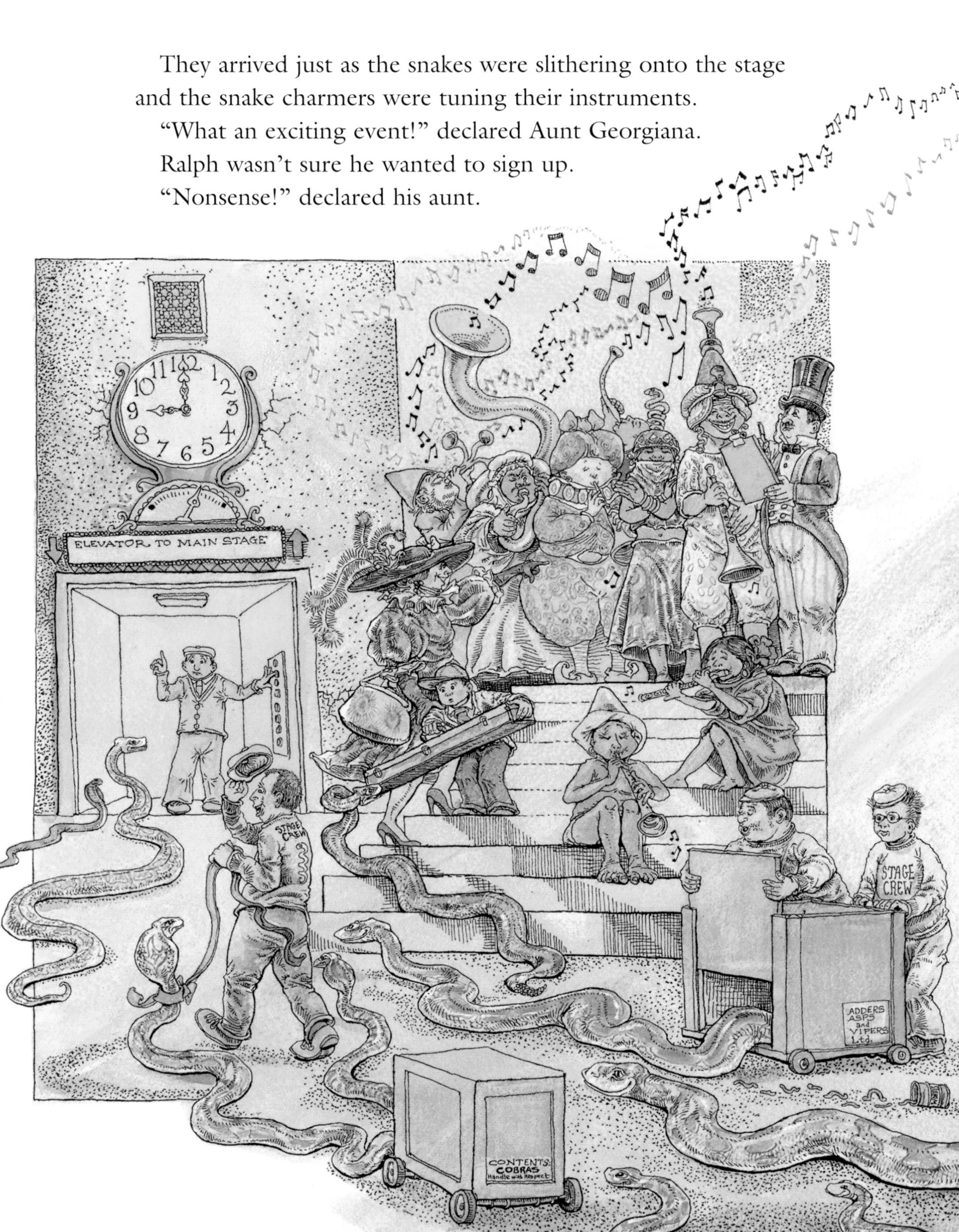

Many of the contestants ran into difficulty, but when Ralph played, all the snakes danced to his music.

Ralph's success gave Aunt Georgiana another idea.

Discovering that a sea serpent was causing problems for the navy, she ran to the telephone.

She promised the admiral that her talented nephew would be able to charm the serpent.

The admiral came at once to meet Ralph and to show him slides of the monster in action.

Ralph was worried. He decided that he needed a secret weapon ready in case of trouble.

Much later aboard the admiral's gunboat Ralph nervously began to play.

Attracted to the music, the monster rose to the surface and snatched the bassoon.

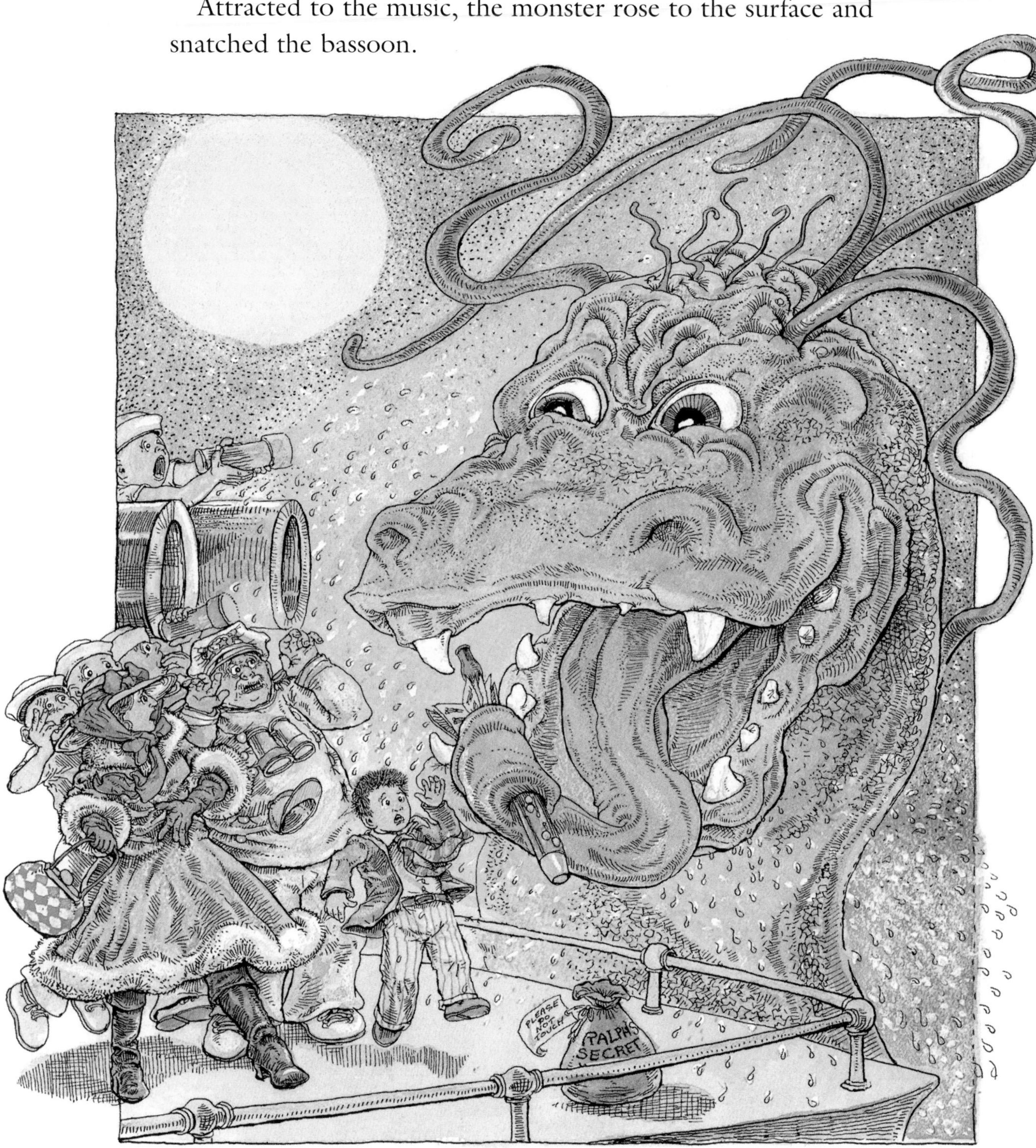

When the music stopped, the sea serpent became angry with Ralph. The crew was frantic. The admiral seemed confused.

"Do something! Save my nephew!" shrieked Aunt Georgiana.

"If we fire, we'll blast Ralph to bits!" wailed the admiral. "What shall we do?"

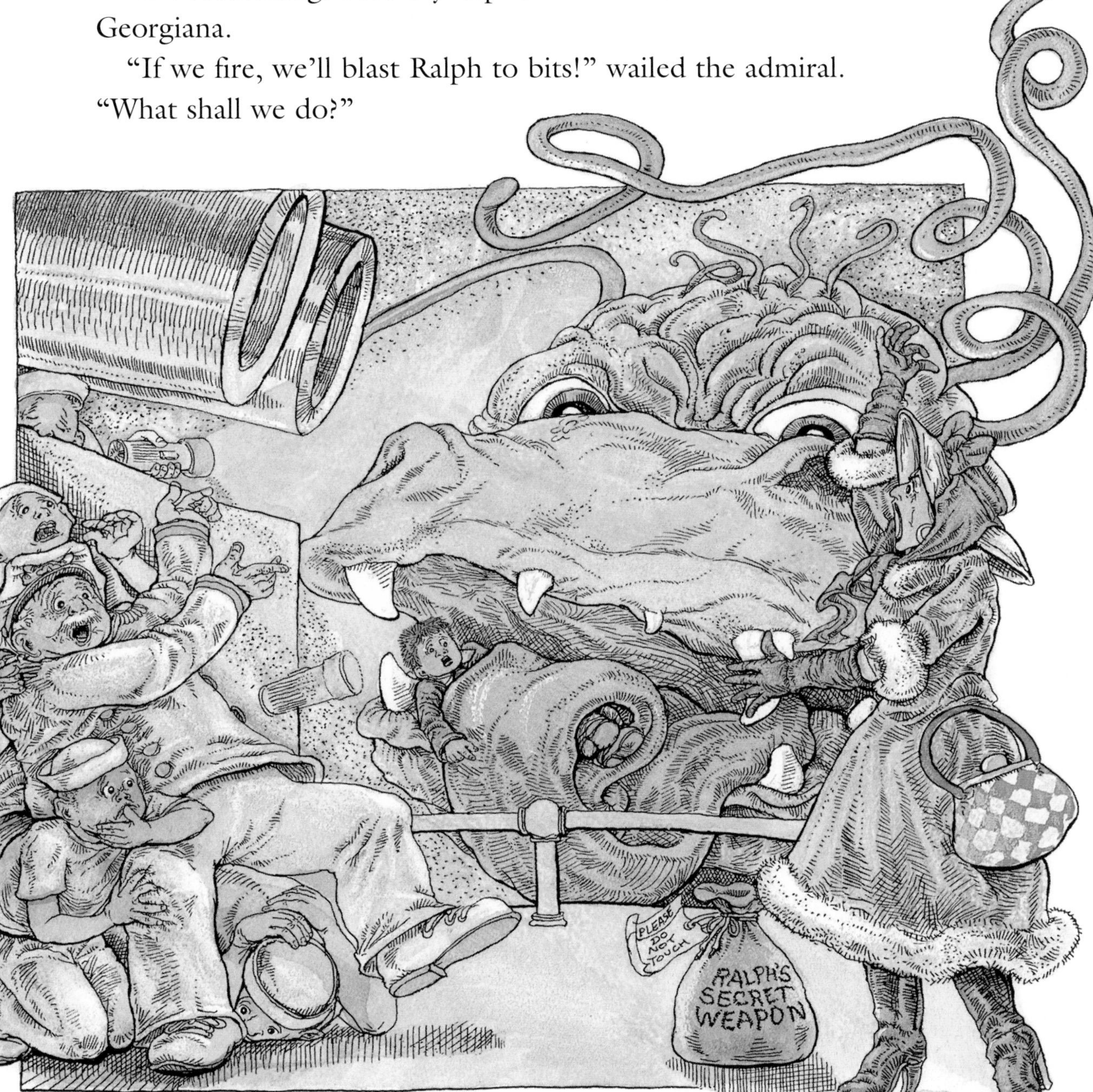

"Throw my secret weapon!" cried Ralph.

Aunt Georgiana bounded across the deck and flung the bag into the monster's throat.

It sank back making strange burbling sounds.

Suddenly a thunderous hiccup blasted Ralph and the other victims to freedom.

"What was in that bag?" cried Aunt Georgiana.

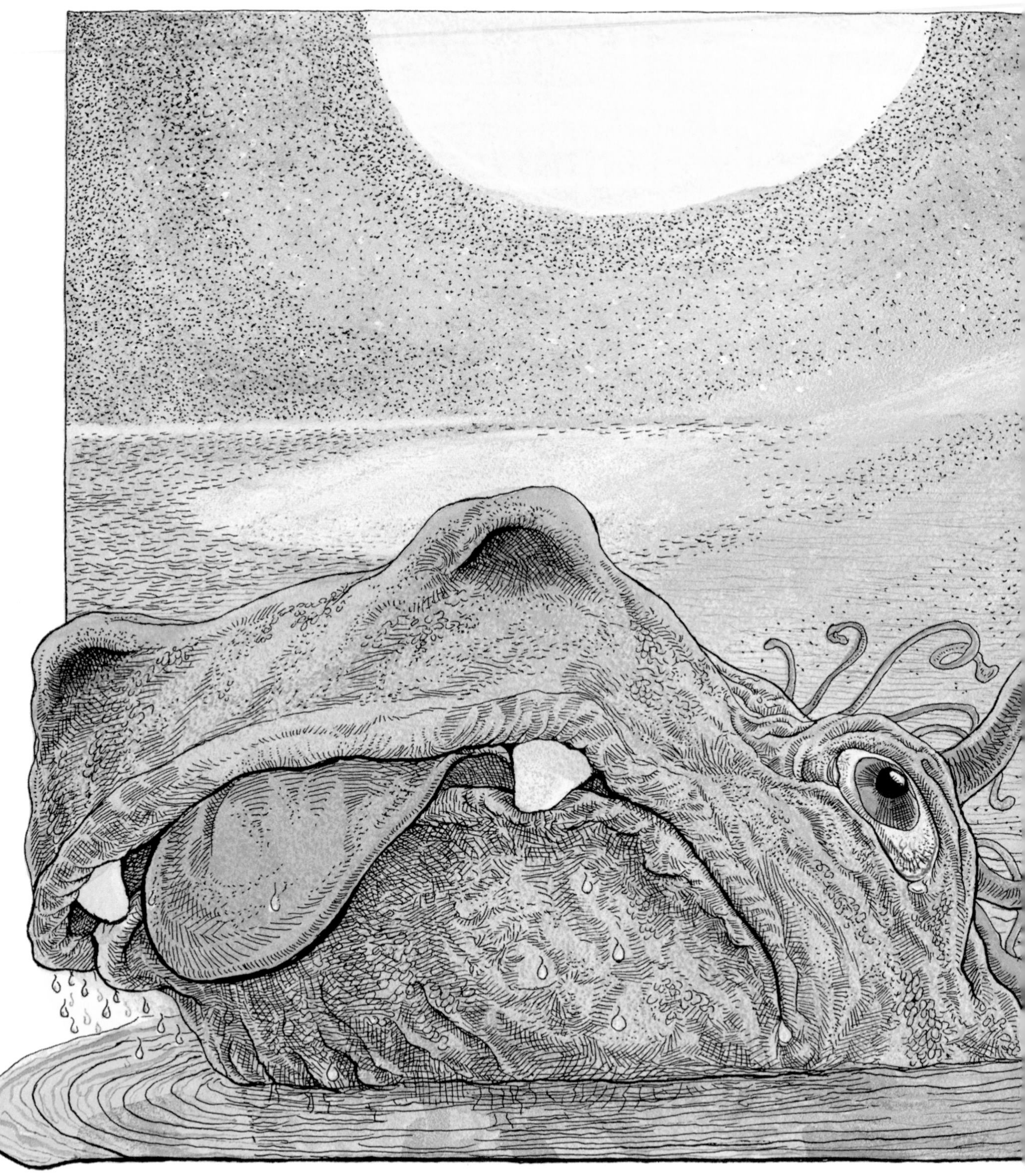

"Your cake," replied Ralph.

When they finally returned home, Aunt Georgiana was exhausted. Ralph was tired too. He announced that he was giving up the bassoon forever.

Aunt Georgiana did not object.

For the rest of the summer Aunt Georgiana kept busy with her projects, while Ralph went swimming, played with the Great Danes, reread his favorite books, and rested up for the fourth grade.

Best Friends

• 1986 •

Louise Jenkins and I love horses, but we aren't allowed to have real ones.

I said, "Let's pretend that a stallion named Golden Silverwind lives in a stable between our houses." Louise loved the idea.

At school we pushed our desks together.

And we played on the same team.

At lunch we shared our chocolate milk.

Chocolate is Louise's favorite, and it's mine too.

After school we pretended that we rode Golden Silverwind. Our magic witch hats gave us the power to make our neighborhood anything we wanted it to be.

And after dark, when it seemed to be haunted, we weren't scared as long as we were together.

We were best friends.

Summer came, and so did Louise's aunt and uncle. They took her to a mountain resort for a vacation. Louise told me that she didn't want to go. "It will be awful," she said. "And I'll miss you every day."

When she left, our neighborhood turned into a lonely desert.

If only Louise would be able to escape.

I even wished she'd get a contagious disease so they'd have to let her come home.

I wouldn't be afraid of catching it. I'd nurse her back to health with chocolate milk.

I missed her so much! I wished that Golden Silverwind and I could rescue her!

Finally I got a postcard. It said:

Dear Kathy,

This place is terrific. Yesterday I saw three deer behind the lodge. There are lots of kids my age, and Aunt Pat and Uncle Bart take us camping on Pine Cone Peak. I hope you're having fun too.

Love from your friend,
Louise

Later I heard Mrs. Jenkins say that Louise had made lots of new friends and was having the best summer of her life.

It wasn't fair. She wasn't lonely like me. She wasn't missing me at all.

Louise Jenkins was a traitor! She was my *worst* friend.

I wished that a volcanic eruption would blast Pine Cone Peak into pebbles.

Mom told me not to be jealous of Louise's new friends.

Later she said, "I heard that the house across the street has been sold. Maybe there'll be someone your age in the new family."

I prayed for fifty kids my age. Fifty new best friends with *real* horses!

When the moving man came, I asked him, "How many people in the new family?"

He said, "One."

I asked if it was someone my age.

He said, "Nope, it's Mr. Jode. He's seventy-two."

This was the worst summer of my life! The new family was one old man!

Mom said we should be good neighbors, and she sent me to invite Mr. Jode for a cookout.

When he saw my witch hat he said, "I wish you'd use your magic powers to help me find good homes for the new puppies that Sarah is expecting."

I ran home to ask Mom if I could have one. She said yes.

I couldn't wait to have a puppy of my own. And if Louise Jenkins wanted to play with it after she got back from Pine Cone Peak, I'd say, "NEVER!" That would fix her.

Mr. Jode and I talked about how much fun it would be when the puppies were born. I told him I wanted a spotted one just like Sarah.

"The first spotted one will be yours," he promised.

One day Mrs. Jenkins showed up and said, "I understand that your dog is expecting puppies. I'd like to reserve one for my daughter, Louise."

I couldn't stand to think of Louise having one of Sarah's puppies. I told Mr. Jode that I would keep all of them.

Mr. Jode said, "Three years ago Sarah had eight puppies in one litter. Would your mother want that many dogs?"

I had to admit that eight dogs would drive my mom crazy.

Mr. Jode asked me if I was afraid that Louise wouldn't give her puppy a good home.

I had to admit that she would.

A week later Louise came back. Her mother had already told her that we were both getting puppies, and she was all excited about us raising them together.

Next she started talking about all the campouts on Pine Cone Peak, and how her uncle and aunt had already planned a return trip for the following summer.

I pretended to be very interested in my book.

Then she told me that she was glad to be home, and that she had missed me very much.

She had brought me a red Pine Cone Peak sweatshirt, a sparrow's feather, and a whistle on a lanyard that she had woven herself.

I told her how much I'd missed her. But I didn't tell her how mad I had been.

I took Louise to meet my new friends. I knew that they would all like each other, and they did. I said, "Aren't Sarah's spots beautiful? I'm going to get the first puppy that looks like her."

A few nights later Mr. Jode called to say that Sarah was having her puppies.

By the time we arrived, one puppy had already been born. It was brown. Mr. Jode handed him to Louise, saying, "When he grows up, he'll look just like Sarah's mother."

Sarah went to sleep. Mr. Jode and Louise made hot chocolate and tried to think of a name for her puppy. I couldn't wait for mine to be born.

Sarah slept for hours. Finally Mr. Jode said, "It looks like there's only one puppy this time. Sarah has never had such a small litter before."

I felt awful.

It wasn't fair! Louise got to spend the whole summer camping on Pine Cone Peak, and now she had Sarah's only puppy.

Louise said, "I think the brown puppy should belong to both of us. We could name him Golden Silverwind."

Mr. Jode said, “I’ll build him a doghouse between your houses.

“And Sarah and I will help with his training.”

When I got home, I kept thinking how lucky I was to have a special friend like Louise. I was already worried about how much I would miss her when she went away next summer.

But at least this time when she's camping on Pine Cone Peak, I'll have Golden Silverwind all to myself.

The Christmas Witch

• 1992 •

Madame Pestilence expected her students at the Academy for Young Goblins and Witches to scowl at all times. It was one of the many rules that Gloria had trouble remembering.

Every time Madame Pestilence spotted Gloria passing her office, she would holler, "STOP SMILING!"

It was easy to scowl at dinnertime because the same awful creamed cockroach casserole was served every night. It made all of the students sick.

"Stop complaining!" Madame Pestilence would snarl. "This diet will turn you into wicked witches and goblins—as mean as your headmistress."

One evening at midnight the students were marched to broom drill. They chanted a chorus of magic phrases, and WHOOSH! WHOOSH! WHOOSH! The brooms snapped into take-off position and shot toward the moon.

One broom, however, refused to budge.

As usual Gloria had muddled the magic phrases. Madame Pestilence was furious. "Copy the first nine hundred and ninety-nine pages of the *Encyclopedia of Spells and Curses* nine hundred and ninety-nine times!" she screamed.

Madame Pestilence rocketed skyward, and Gloria was left alone.

Gloria was wearily at work on her assignment when suddenly she heard the tinkling of bells.

Following the sound, she went down a winding staircase and passed through a small doorway she'd never noticed before. There she discovered a storytelling circle where a stranger was reading a book called *A Magic Tale of Christmas.*

The story enchanted Gloria and filled her with joyful holiday visions. "I want to be a Christmas witch!" she cried.

"Christmas magic can bring about miracles," said Gloria's new friend. "But sometimes it takes courage and imagination to make Christmas wishes come true."

Summoning all the courage and imagination she could, Gloria cried, "I wish for a wonderful Christmas adventure!"

The next thing Gloria knew she was flying through the night. "On that dark planet you'll find the polka-dotted Pepperwills and the striped Valdoons," said her friend. "They have a great need of Christmas magic."

She waved good-bye, and Gloria found herself slowly falling.

As Gloria passed through the clouds, she could see the walls that separated the lands of Valdoon and Pepperwill. In the woods between them she spotted the ruins of a castle.

Gloria landed among the striped soldiers. “It’s a Pepperwill spy!” they cried. “Seize her!”

“I’m a friend,” protested Gloria. “I’ve come to plan a Christmas celebration for the Valdoons and the Pepperwills.”

“That’s absurd!” cried the soldiers. “Ever since the castle blew up in the War of 1382, we Valdoons have hated the Pepperwills. Our feud will last forever!”

Across the valley Gloria was confronted by the Pepperwills. They repeated the story of the castle and the feud.

Like the Valdoons, the Pepperwills were not interested in Gloria's plans for Christmas. "We wouldn't dare leave our walls," they declared. "At any moment the Valdoons might attack."

These Pepperwills and Valdoons are almost as gloomy as goblins and witches, thought Gloria. She set off into the woods to explore the castle ruins.

If I rebuild the castle, it will cheer up the Valdoons and the Pepperwills, she thought. Then it will be the perfect spot for a Christmas celebration!

She set off to work, but she soon realized that the job was too much for her. "I'll never be able to finish by Christmas," she said, sobbing.

That night she dreamed that her friend from the storytelling circle came to comfort her.

As the dream ended, Gloria was awakened by the sound of tinkling bells and the arrival of elfin visitors. "We're from the North Pole," they explained. "We've come to help."

For the rest of the night the castle hummed and clattered with the sounds of construction.

Before leaving, one of the elves gave Gloria a recipe for a magic Christmas cake. "Mix these ingredients every day with love and generosity," he said. "By Christmas your cake will be irresistible!"

When the Valdoons and Pepperwills woke up, they were amazed to see the restored castle—and banners inviting everyone to a grand-opening party.

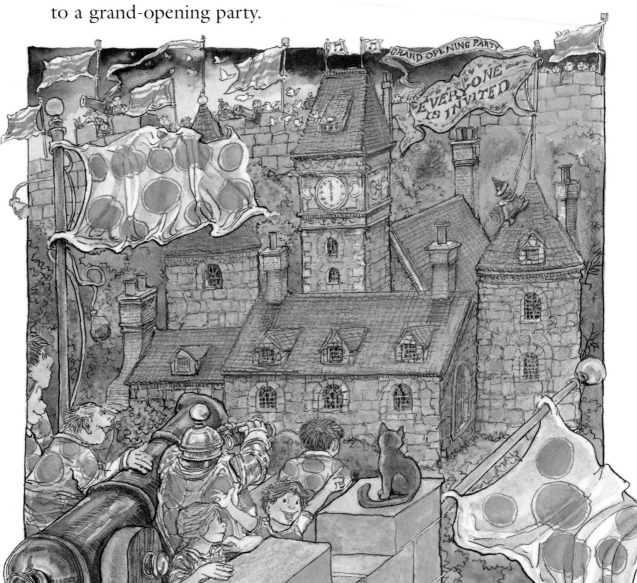

Gloria waited all day for her guests to arrive.
But no one came.

At sunset Gloria went to see the Valdoons. "Why didn't you come to my party?" she asked.

"Because you invited those horrid Pepperwills!" they declared.

On the Pepperwill side of the valley things weren't much brighter. "Celebrate with those dreadful Valdoons?" they cried. "NEVER! NEVER! NEVER! NEVER!"

Gloria thought for a minute. "All right," she announced. "Mondays, Wednesdays, and Fridays will be Pepperwill days at the castle."

The Pepperwills cheered.

Across the valley the Valdoons were equally delighted to hear the castle would be theirs on Tuesdays, Thursdays, and Saturdays.

Dividing the week between the enemies worked very well.

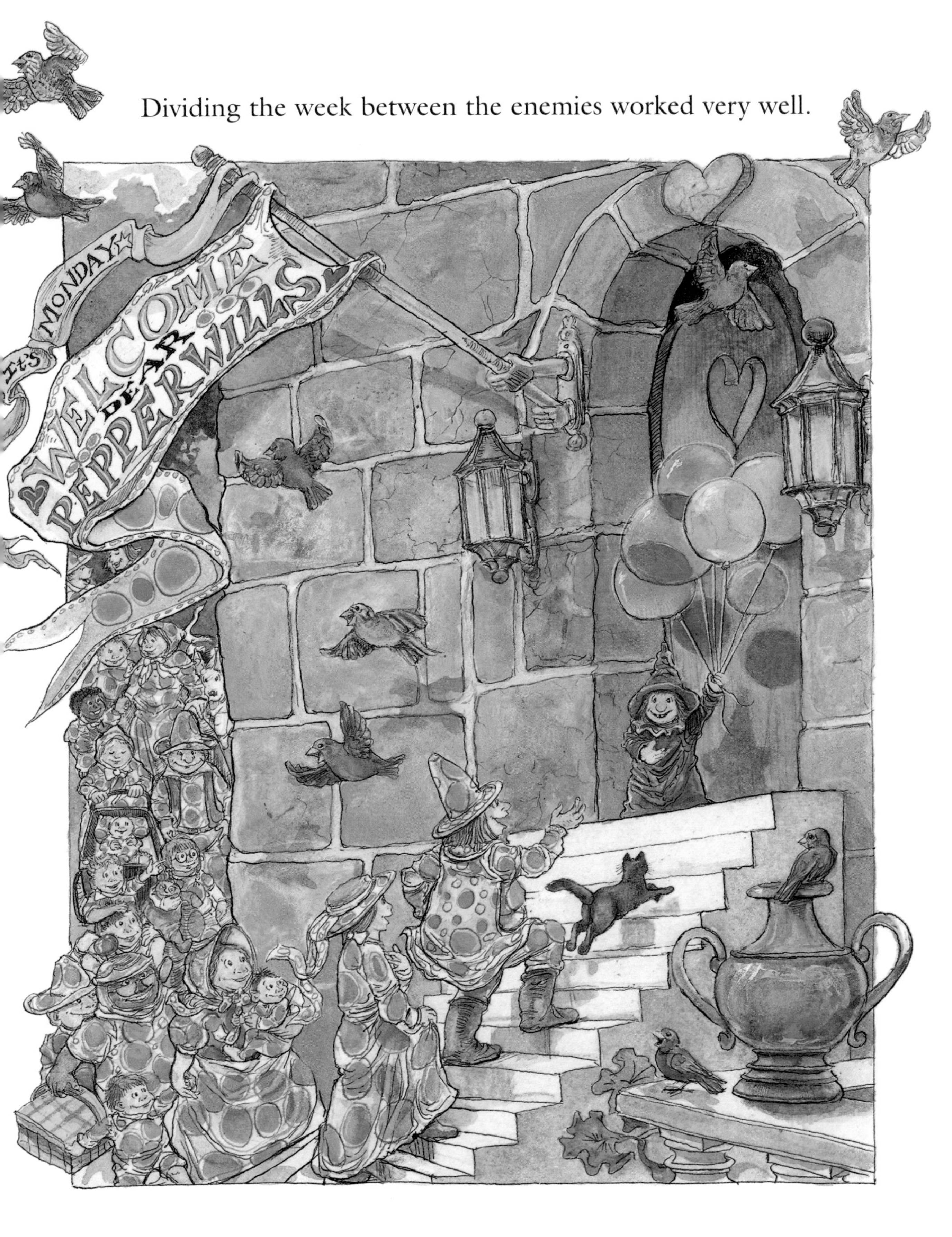

Everyone loved the way Gloria and the elves had rebuilt the castle, and as the days passed, it rang with the sounds of fun and frolic.

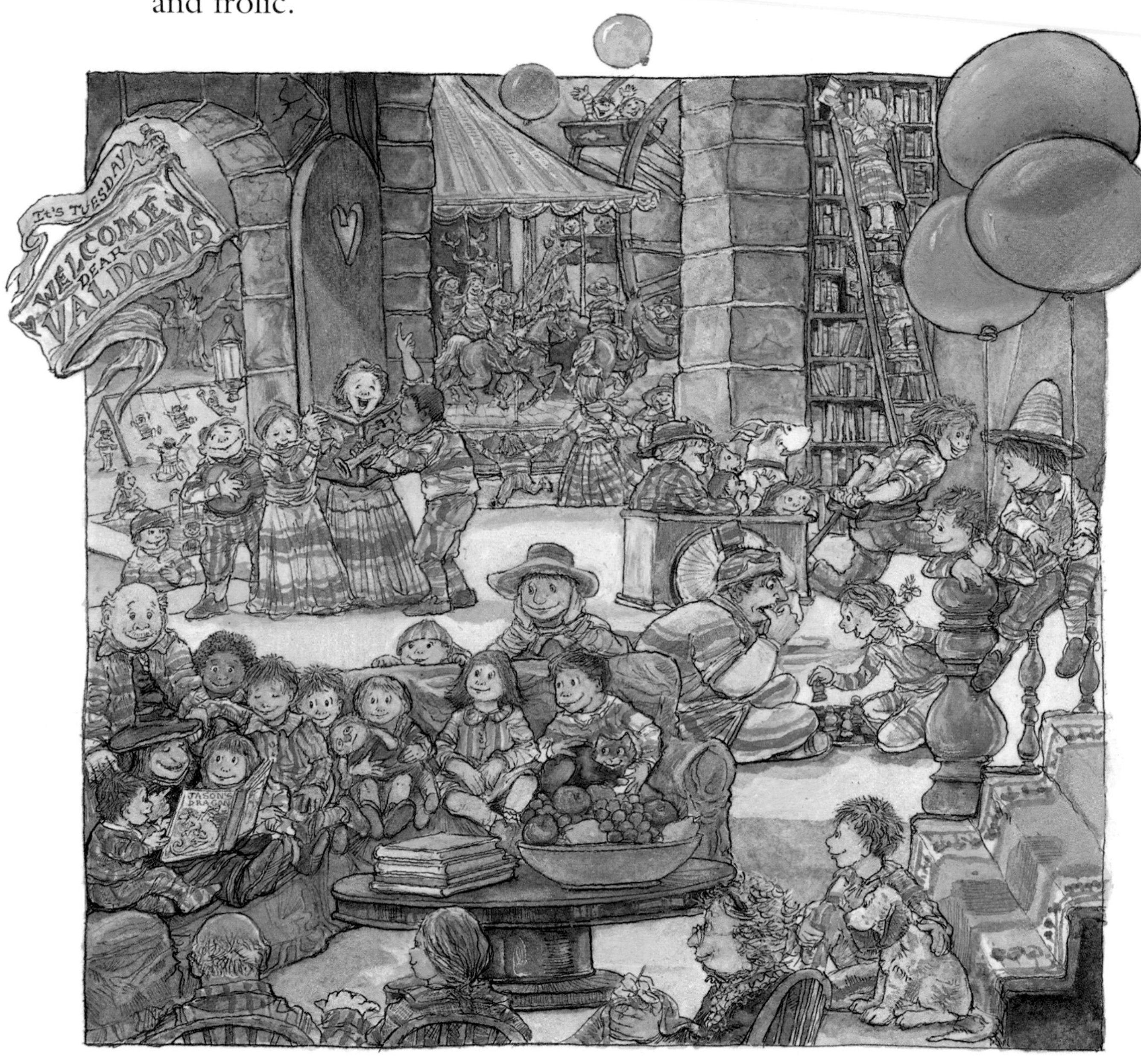

Before long both groups came to think of Gloria as a very special friend.

All this happiness drove away the gloomy clouds that had surrounded the planet for centuries. Soon the change was noticed by a band of patrolling witches. They swooped down to investigate.

Madame Pestilence was at the head of the formation. “So,” she muttered, “our little Gloria is the culprit! We shall have our revenge!” A goblin spy was immediately sent to the castle.

Night after night the spy watched Gloria mixing and stirring the ingredients for her Christmas cake.

One Pepperwill morning in December Gloria bounced out of bed with a joyous whoop. She had thought of an idea to end the feud! Christmas was to be on a Sunday that year, and she announced a gala masquerade party at the castle.

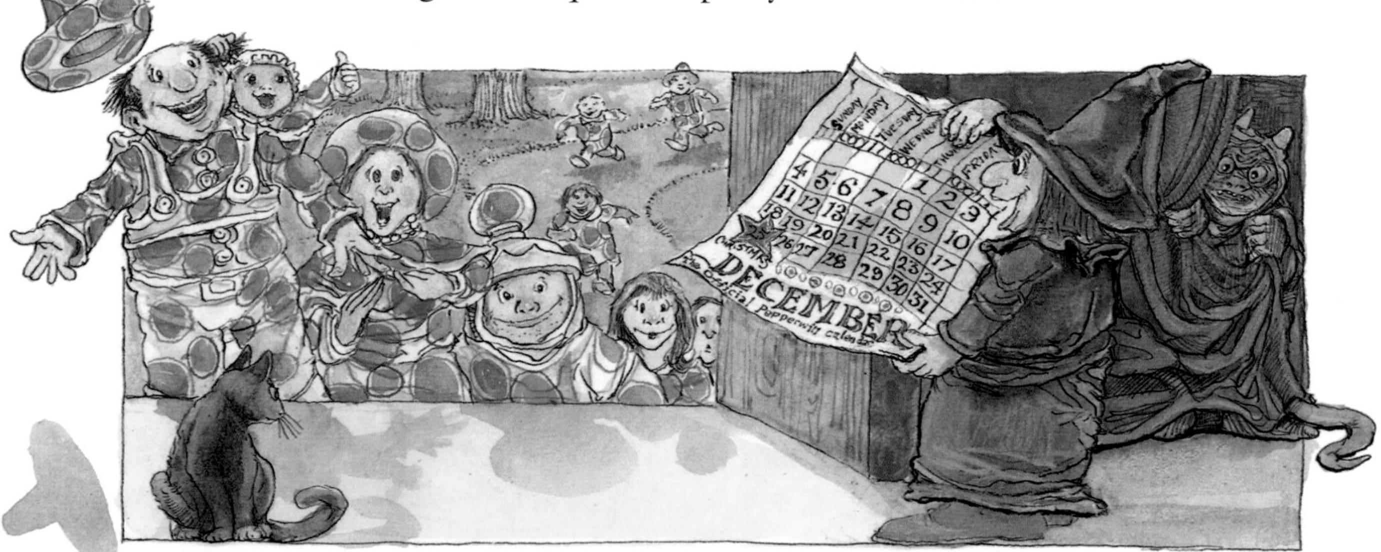

The next day the Valdoons heard the same news.

However, neither the Valdoons nor the Pepperwills were told that their enemies had also been invited.

The elves arrived to help everyone make costumes. Gloria baked dozens of cookies, pies, and puddings while she continued to work on her cake.

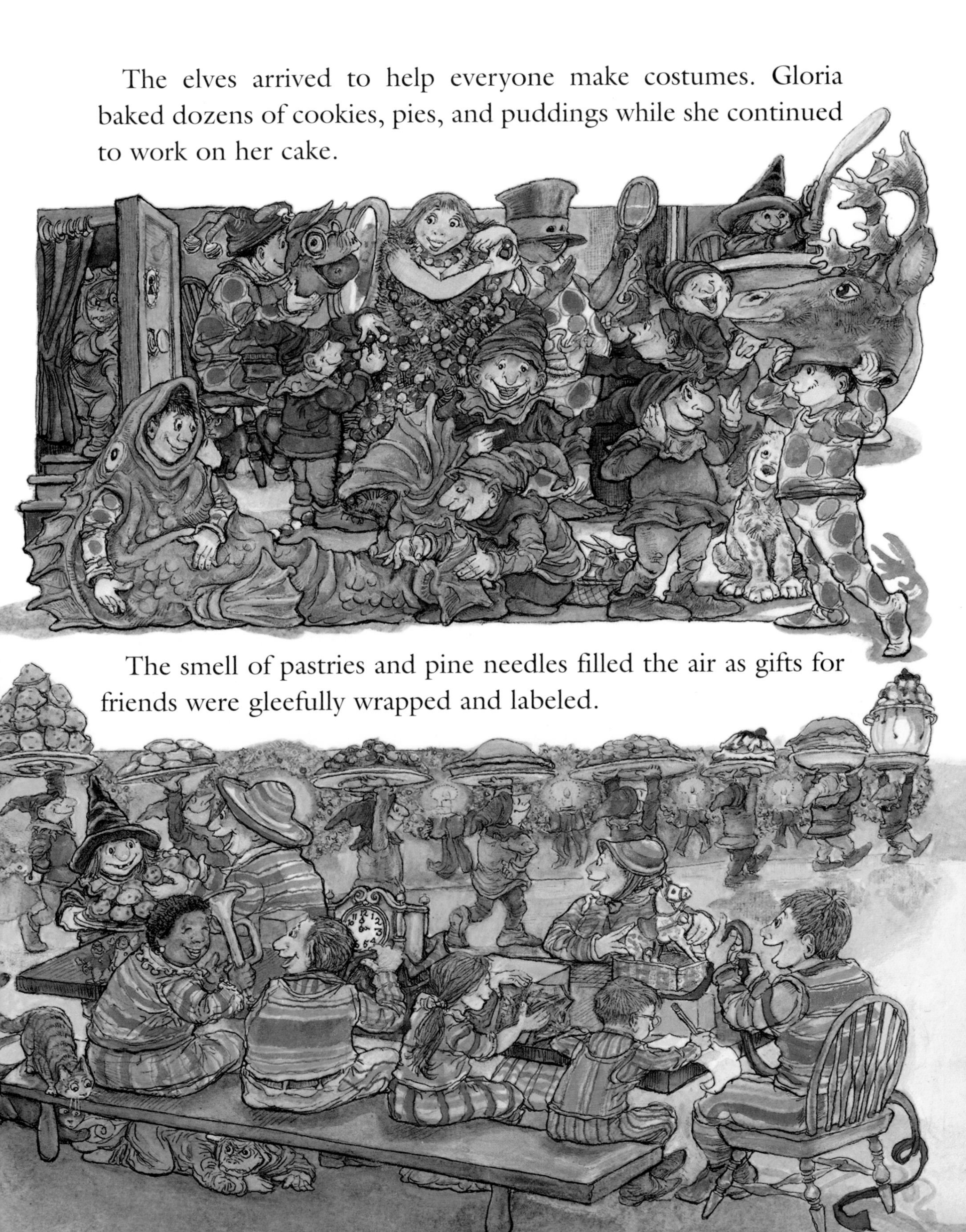

The smell of pastries and pine needles filled the air as gifts for friends were gleefully wrapped and labeled.

On Christmas Eve Gloria's cake was finally finished. "It's a masterpiece!" cried the elves. "Let's keep it hidden until after tomorrow's dinner, and then we'll have a grand presentation!"

Before going to bed they changed the labels on all the gifts so each Pepperwill present would seem to come from a Valdoon, and each gift for a Valdoon would seem to come from a Pepperwill.

Meanwhile the goblin spy had slipped out of the castle. He broomed toward the academy at top speed.

No sooner had the witches and goblins assembled and the spy's report been heard, than Madame Pestilence began pounding the great war gong. "Gloria's Christmas plot must be squelched immediately," she bellowed. "Here are your orders:

"ONE! Go to the castle and destroy Gloria's cake.

"TWO! Remain hidden under the cake cover until it is raised, and then CHARGE!

"THREE! Throw Gloria and the elves into the dungeon and chase the others back to their walls.

"GO AT ONCE!"

The attackers landed at the castle and quickly demolished the unguarded cake. From beneath the cover there came a muffled chorus of ooooohs, aaaaahs, and hmmmmms, followed by several hours of intense whispering.

Just before dawn, when all was quiet, Madame Pestilence slipped into the castle and hid behind the curtains.

On Christmas morning the costumed Pepperwills and Valdoons mingled and exchanged greetings without suspicion. Together they made their way through the falling snow and into Gloria's welcoming arms.

What a jolly time they had dancing, singing carols, and decorating the tree.

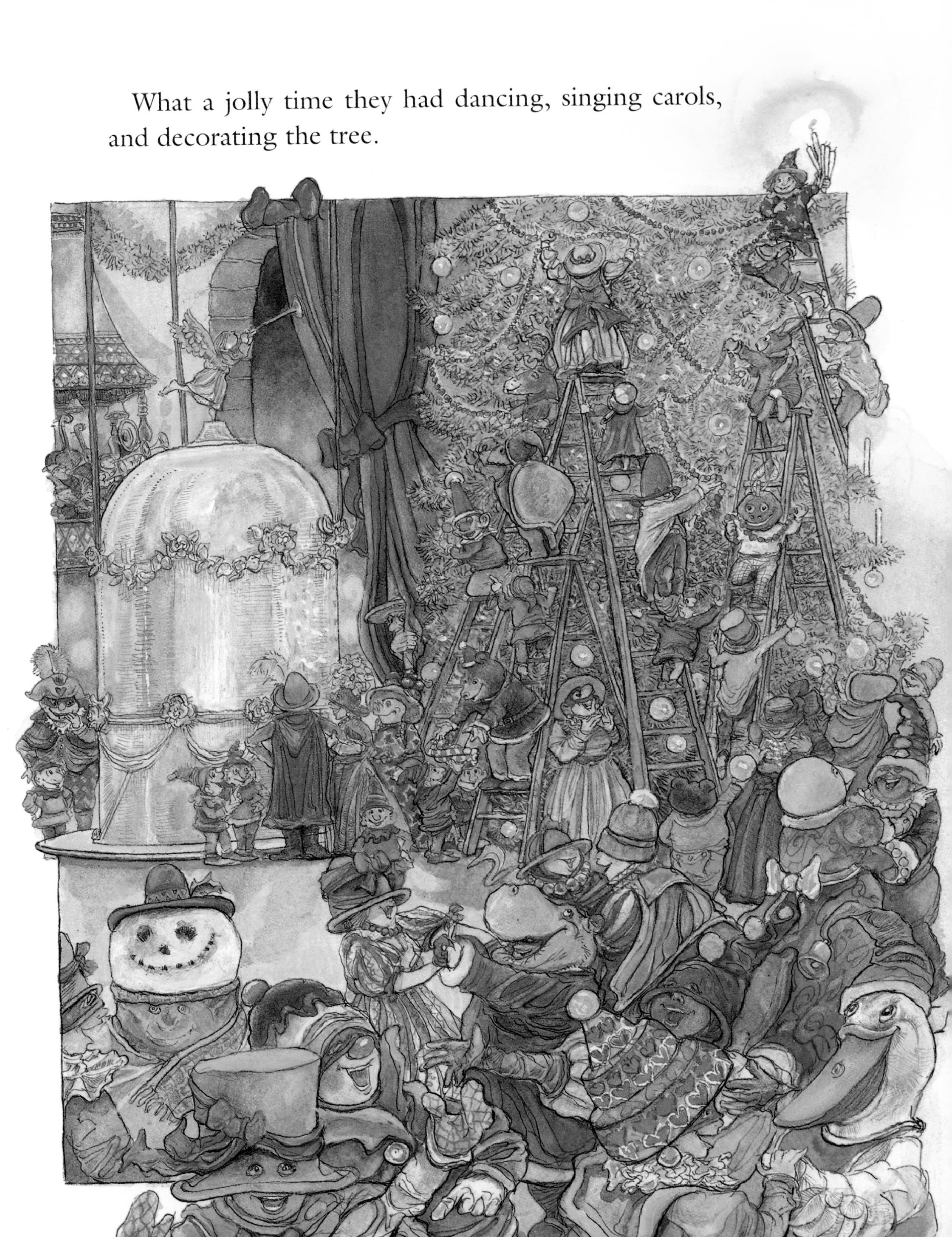

After the feast Gloria exclaimed, "Open your presents and take off your masks! MERRY CHRISTMAS TO ALL!"

The Valdoons and the Pepperwills were flabbergasted to discover that they had been celebrating and exchanging gifts with their enemies. "How did this happen?" they cried. "Are we under an evil spell?"

But there was no time for answers. A trumpet fanfare sounded and the elves cried, "Hear ye! Hear ye! We now present the great Christmas dessert."

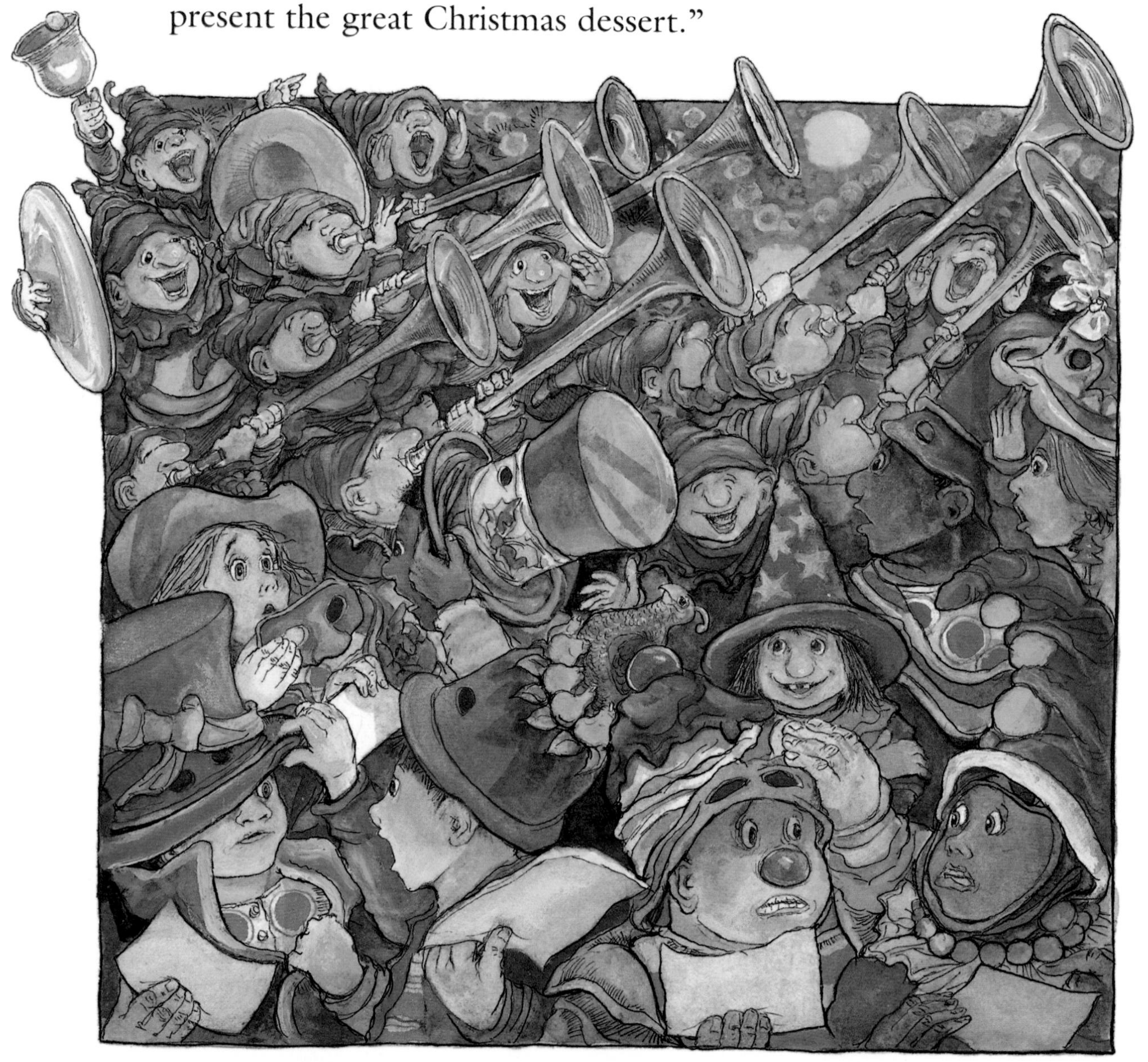

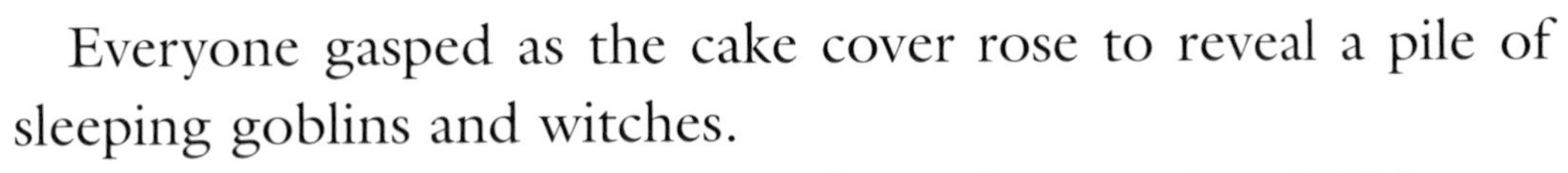

Everyone gasped as the cake cover rose to reveal a pile of sleeping goblins and witches.

Madame Pestilence exploded from the curtains. "Wake up, you lazy louts!" she shrieked. "Remember your orders! Attack! Attack! Attack!"

The students awoke, but instead of obeying, they hollered, "WE QUIT!"

Madame Pestilence was stunned. "You can't quit!" she roared. "It's forbidden! How dare you defy me?"

"Gloria's cake is to blame!" they cried. "It was *delicious*! We will never never NEVER eat creamed cockroach casserole again!"

Madame Pestilence flailed the air with her broom. "IDIOTS! BLOCKHEADS! TRAITORS!" she screamed. "I shall have my revenge!"

Thunder rumbled overhead, and the planet began to tremble. The Pepperwills and the Valdoons were paralyzed with fear.

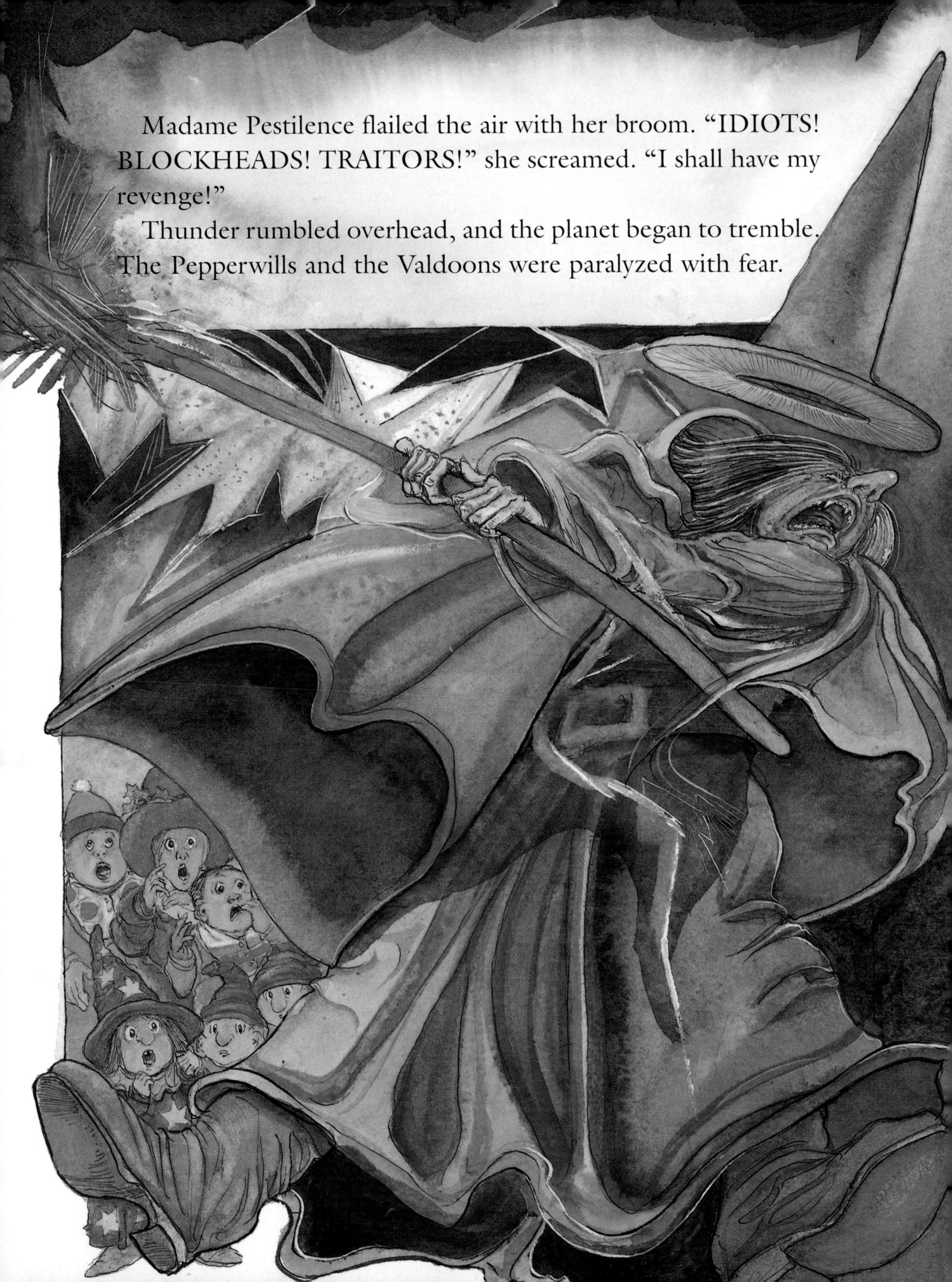

Quickly the elves struck up a joyous Christmas carol. To everyone's amazement a shimmering star arched into the room and hovered above the tree. In the golden light the thundering and trembling ceased, and Madame Pestilence began to shrink.

For several moments her size and shape continued to change. "What's happening?" wailed the Pepperwills and Valdoons.

"She's becoming a cockroach!" exclaimed Gloria.

The witches and goblins cried, "We're free! We're free! Hooray for Gloria!"

All of this was too much for the Pepperwills and the Valdoons. They scrambled to escape from the castle and from one another.

Gloria hurried after her fleeing friends. "There is nothing to be afraid of!" she cried. "Don't go!"

"If the feud continues," warned the elves, "the planet will darken and Madame Pestilence will reappear."

The old enemies stopped and slowly turned around. "Please stay!" pleaded Gloria. "Remember how happy you were when the magic of Christmas entered your hearts?"

For several moments the Valdoons and Pepperwills stared at one another in silence. Then suddenly they felt ashamed of their long and bitter feud. "Our walls will come down," they said quietly. "And from this time onward we will be neighbors and friends in the united land of Pepperdoon."

All that night while the Christmas celebration continued, the planet of the Pepperdoons glowed more brilliantly that it ever had before.

Library Lil

by Suzanne Williams

• 1997 •

I bet you think all librarians are mousy little old ladies. Hair rolled up in a bun. Beady eyes peering out at you over the tops of those funny half-glasses. An index finger permanently attached to lips mouthing "Shhh."

Bet you never heard about Library Lil.

Lil wasn't always a librarian, of course. She was a kid first, just like most people.

And like most kids, Lil had a wild imagination. She loved to read, and she imagined herself the hero of every book she checked out of the library. By the time she was eight, she'd read all the books in the children's room.

Yes, Lil was a fast reader. And she had the most powerful, strong arms too. When the third-grade soccer ball got stuck under the principal's car, Lil retrieved it.

Her strength might have come from carrying all those books around, for when Lil ran out of children's books, she started in on encyclopedias.

She used to check out a whole set at once. She'd walk down the street reading the "A" volume, held open in one hand, while she balanced the remaining volumes on the palm of the other hand. She turned pages with her teeth.

ENCYCLOPEDIA
ATOMIC

So it was no surprise to anyone when Lil grew up and became a librarian, landing a job in the nearby town of Chesterville. The townspeople soon dubbed her Library Lil.

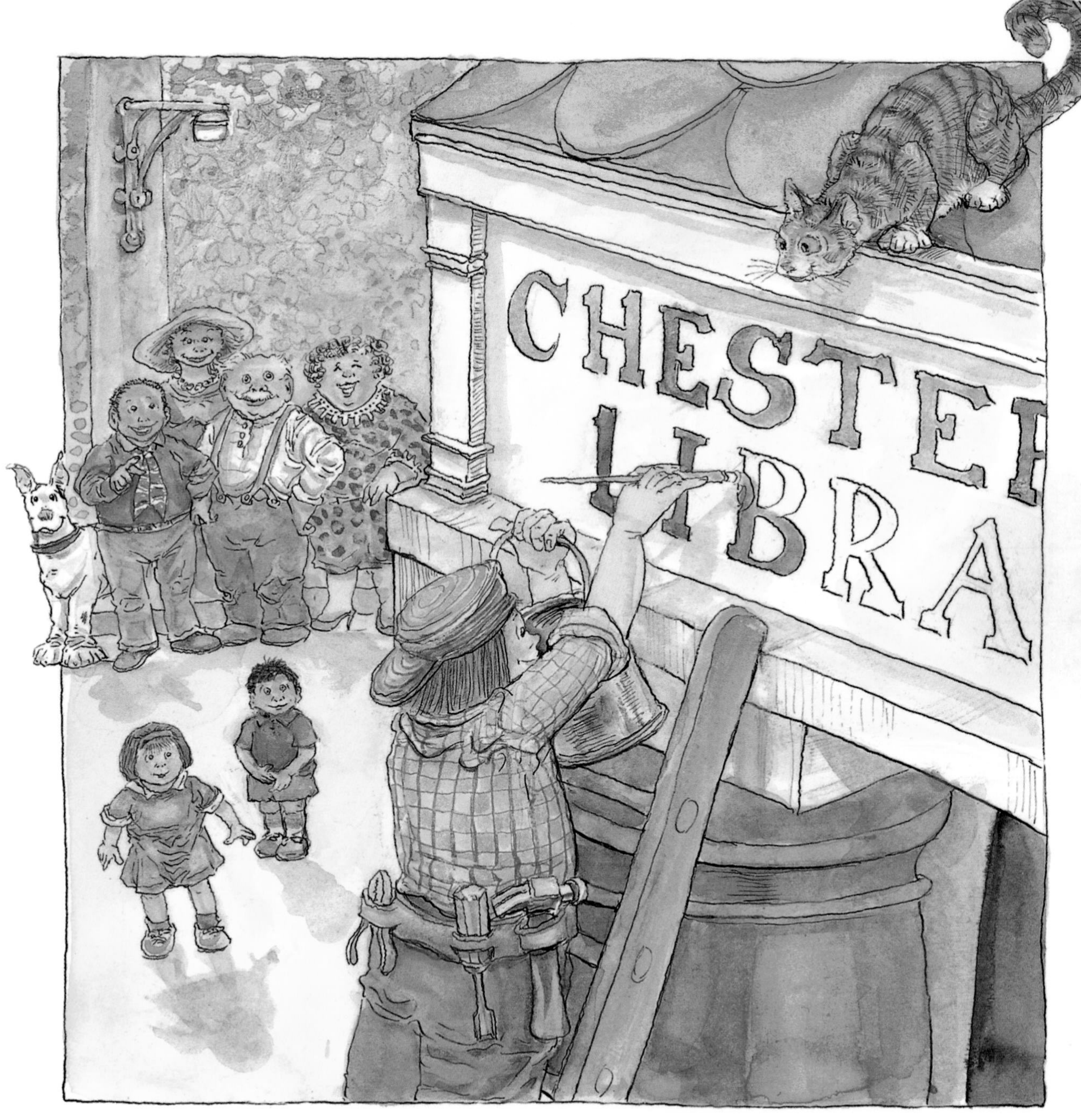

Lil's specialty was storytelling, but when she advertised a storytime in the local newspaper, no one showed up. And when she posted a list of fantastic new books she had ordered, no one came to check them out.

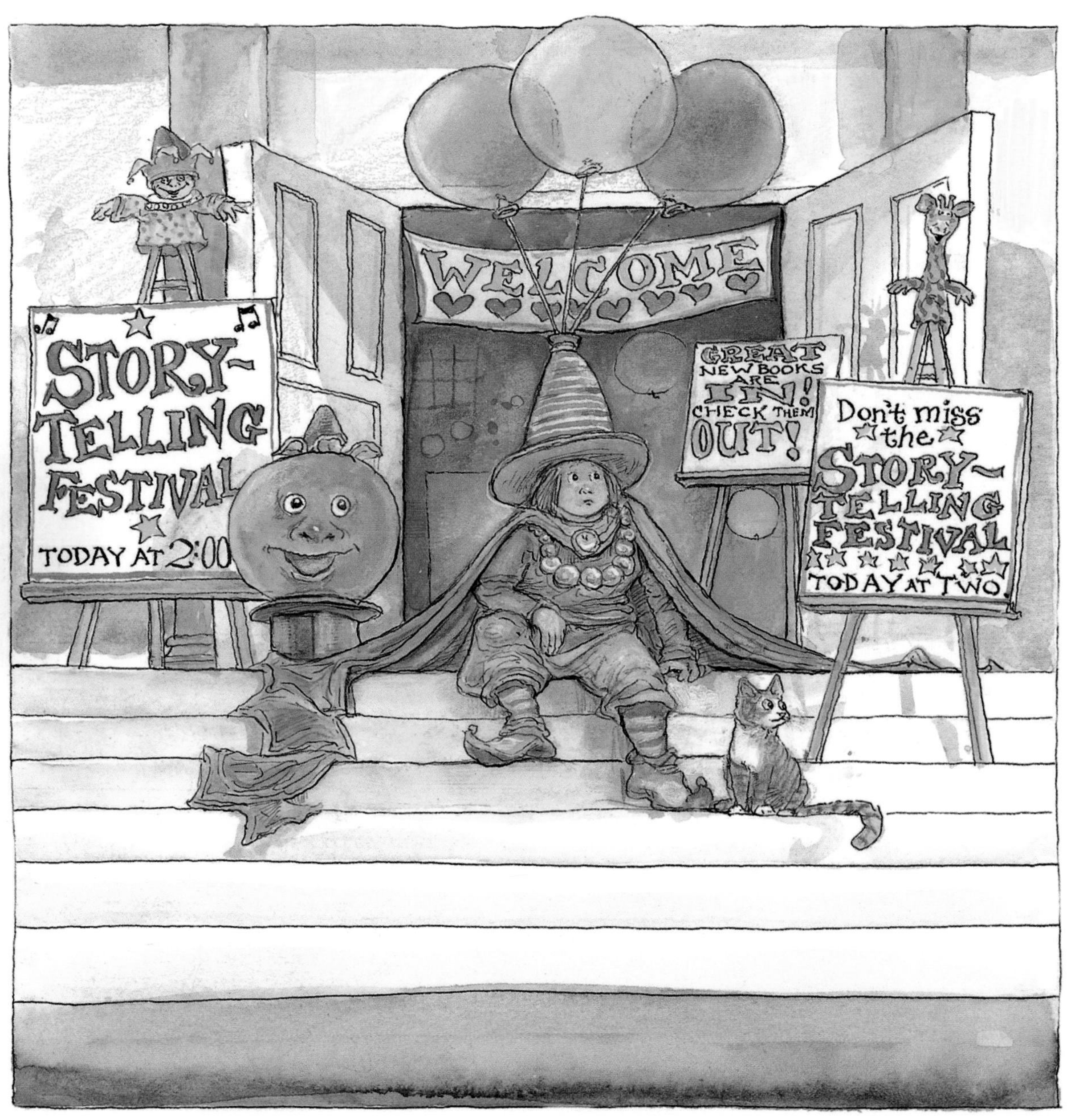

It was clear that the people of Chesterville were not avid readers. Television was their favorite form of entertainment, and Lil did not approve of TV. "Devil's Invention," she called it. "Keeps folks away from good books."

To Lil's way of thinking, TV was an evil that ranked right up there with poison ivy and mosquitoes. She knew she had her work cut out for her.

One horrible, stormy night the wind blew down some power lines. The whole town of Chesterville was plunged into darkness. TVs popped off like flashbulbs.

This was the chance Lil had been waiting for.

She fought her way through the driving rain to the town's ancient bookmobile, battling eighty-mile-per-hour winds that threatened to carry her away like a feather in an updraft.

Unfortunately that old bookmobile had been sitting idle too long. Its battery was deader than a pickled herring. But did that stop Library Lil? No, sir! Up and down the streets of town she went, pushing that bookmobile ahead of her just like a baby carriage.

By the end of the night every man, woman, and child in Chesterville was reading a book by the flickering light of a candle. The power was out for two whole weeks, by which time the townspeople had solidly formed the habit of reading.

Suddenly folks were borrowing more books than they had in the entire fifty years since the library had been built. And there was standing room only for Lil's storytimes.

Not long after the storm, a motorcycle gang rode into town. The leader of the gang was Bust-'em-up Bill. He was a towering six foot seven, and when he took off his jacket to play pool, he revealed a skull-and-crossbones tattoo that would scare the wool off a sheep.

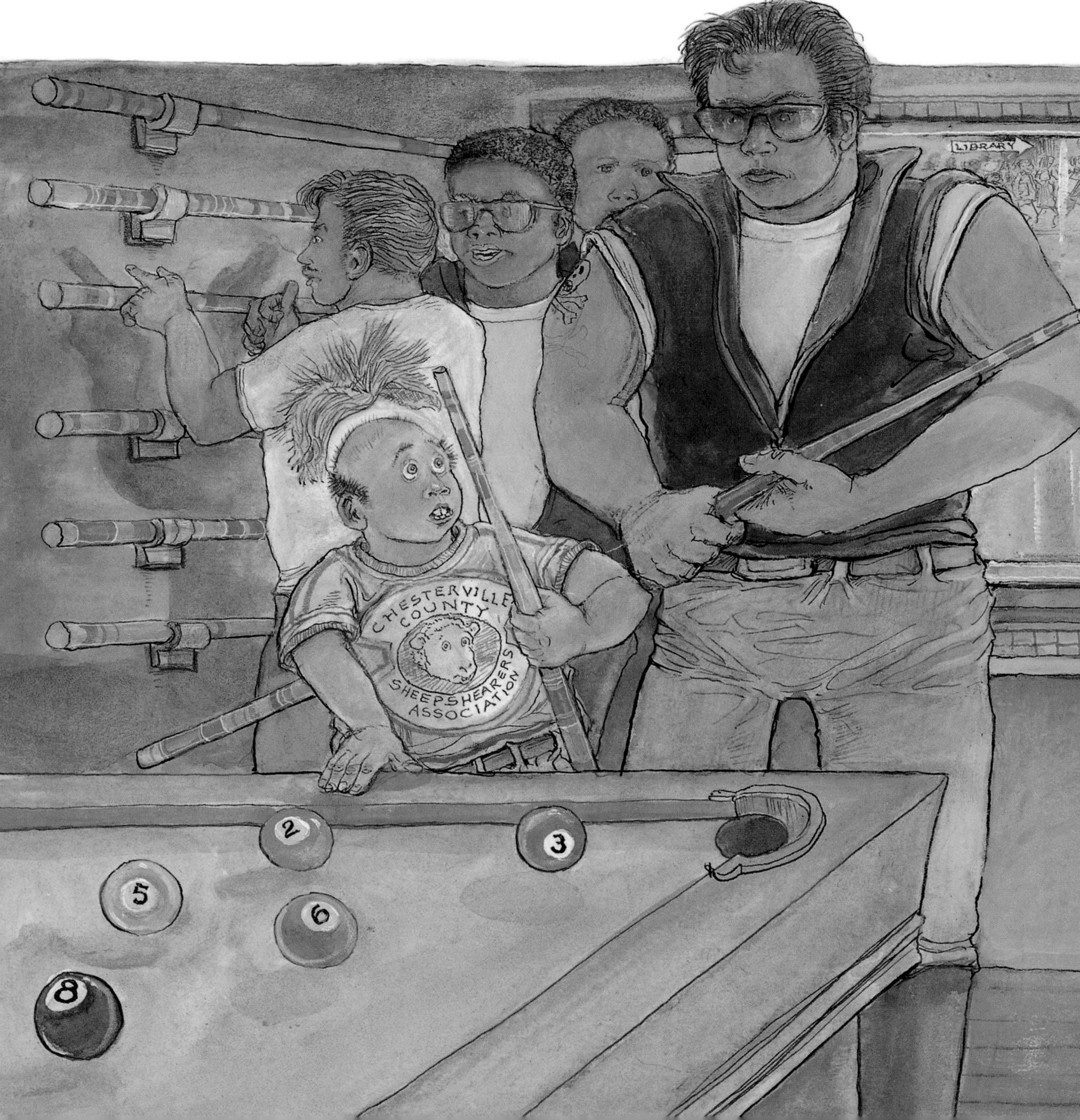

Now, at first Lil took no more notice of Bill and his gang than a duck would of rain. She was only interested in readers, and they kept her plenty busy at the library since the storm. So while Bill and his gang hustled pool at the local tavern, Library Lil checked out books.

It wasn't long before Bust-'em-up Bill found out about Lil, though. You see, he was in the habit of watching professional wrestling on Tuesday nights, so when Tuesday night rolled around, Bill expected to watch his favorite program.

"Where's the danged TV?" he yelled at the bartender.

"Don't have one, sir," said the bartender. "Nobody in town watches it much anymore. Too many good books to read."

"No one around here watches TV?" Bill roared. "What's the matter with you folks?"

The bartender chuckled nervously. "Lil's made us all into readers."

"Readers?" Bill laughed. It was not a pleasant sound. He faced his gang. "Did you hear that? These lily-livered cowards read *books*!" The way he said "books" left no doubt that to him, this was the filthiest word in the English language.

"WHO. IS. LIL?" He spat the words out like bullets.

"Our librarian," squeaked the bartender.

"Where is she?" growled Bill.

The bartender cringed. "She'll be parking her bookmobile across from the library in about ten minutes, sir."

Bill stomped toward the door. "Let's go," he grunted to his gang.

When Lil arrived, she found the parking lot filled with motorcycles and surly bikers. "Move your bikes," she called. "You're blocking my parking place."

"Tough cookies, sister," said Bill. "It's your fault I'm missing my favorite TV show."

"Listen," Lil said. "I don't want trouble. Just move the bikes."

The gang stood their ground.

"All right," said Lil. "If *you* won't move them, I guess I'll just have to move them *for* you."

"Did you hear that?" Bill shouted to his gang. "She'll move them for us. Sister, if you can do that, why I'll, I'll . . ." Bill glanced at the bookmobile. "I'll read a book," he finished. It was the worst thing he could think of.

Lil grinned. She flexed her skinny muscles. Then she stooped down, reaching under one of the motorcycles. Straightening, she suddenly hoisted the motorcycle with one hand and tossed it into the street. It cost her little more effort than flinging an apple core. Bust-'em-up Bill and his gang watched with their jaws hanging down as Lil threw motorcycle after motorcycle onto a stack reaching up toward the moon.

When she'd cleared the parking lot, Lil drove the bookmobile on in. Then she climbed down and headed toward the library's front door.

"All right, boys," she called out. "I'm open for business."

Bill's boys tried to sneak away, but Bill hauled them up by their collars. "Not so fast," he growled. "We're all getting books. If anyone tries to leave without one, he's gonna be reminded why my nickname is Bust-'em-up."

It wasn't long before every man in Bill's gang was reading away. 'Course, some of them hadn't learned too well in school, so Lil gave 'em some easier books to begin on.

Several of the guys got into a fight over who was going to be the first to check out *The Mouse and the Motorcycle.*

Fortunately Lil found some extra copies and calmed things down.

Last time I was over to Chesterville, they'd added a new wing to the town library. Seems Lil's been busier than ever. She's had to take on a library assistant to help out.

The new assistant's a big fellow. The townspeople call him Bookworm Bill.

The kids think he's a whale of a storyteller, but then, he learned from a master.

Since Bill's been on the job, Lil says there hasn't been a single overdue book. I think she's kind of sweet on the guy. Says she's even taken to watching a little of the Devil's Invention—particularly on Tuesday nights.

The Mysterious Tadpole

• 2002 •

"Greetings, nephew!" cried Louis's uncle McAllister. "I've brought a wee bit of Scotland for your birthday."

"Thanks!" said Louis. "Look, Mom and Dad. It's a TADPOLE!"

Louis named him Alphonse and promised to take very good care of him.

Louis took Alphonse to school for show-and-tell.

"Class, here we have a splendid example of a tadpole," exclaimed Ms. Shelbert. "Let's ask Louis to bring it back every week so we can watch it become a frog."

Ms. Shelbert was amazed to see how quickly Alphonse grew. "Maybe it's because he only eats cheeseburgers," said Louis.

When Alphonse became too big for his jar, Louis moved him to the kitchen sink. "He's the perfect pet!" said Louis.

Louis and Alphonse loved to play games.

"Be careful, Louis," said his mother. "The living room is not a soccer field. Something is going to get broken!"

And she was right. That same day the soccer ball slammed into Aunt Tabitha's antique lamp.

"This tadpole is out of control," said Louis's mother. "Something must be done."

"It won't happen again," promised Louis. "I'll take Alphonse to obedience school."

The only animals at the obedience school were dogs. Some of their owners stared at Alphonse suspiciously.

"Pretend you're a dog," whispered Louis.

Alphonse tried to bark, but it sounded like a burp.

"Hold on a minute," said the trainer. "What kind of dog is this?"
"He's a hairless spotted water spaniel from Scotland," explained Louis.

Alphonse quickly learned to SIT, STAY, and RETRIEVE. He graduated at the top of his class.
"My parents will be very pleased," said Louis.

But Louis's parents were not pleased when Alphonse outgrew the sink and had to be moved to the bathtub.

"This shower is too crowded," complained Louis's father. "This bathroom is a mess," moaned Louis's mother.

At least Louis's classmates enjoyed Alphonse, who was still making weekly visits.

"Wow! Show-and-tell is more fun than recess!" they yelled.

But one day Ms. Shelbert decided that Alphonse was not turning into an ordinary frog. She asked Louis to stop bringing him to school.

By the time summer vacation arrived, Alphonse had outgrown the bathtub.

"We could buy the parking lot next door and build him a swimming pool," suggested Louis.

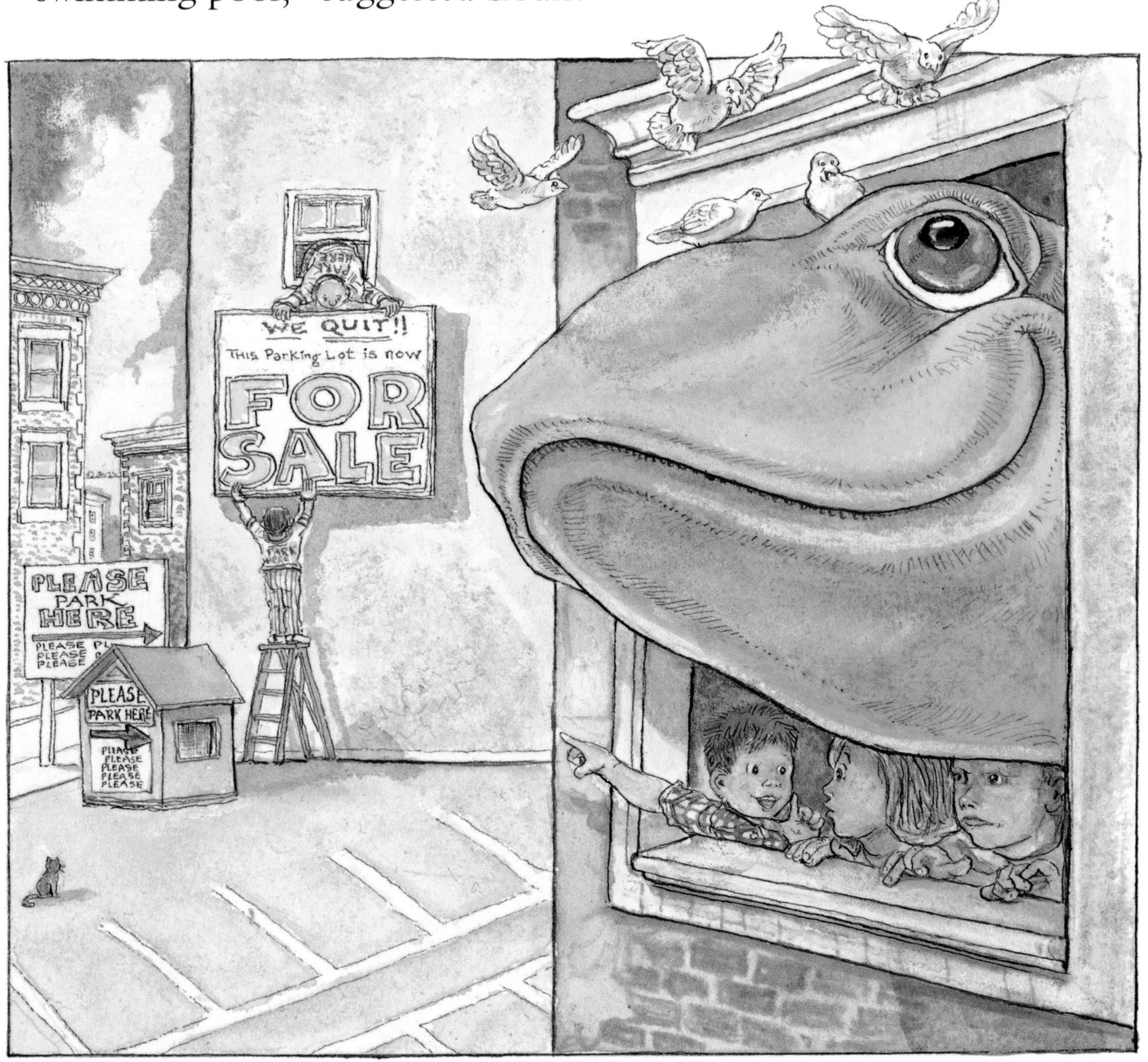

"Be sensible," declared Louis's parents. "Swimming pools are expensive. We're sorry, Louis, but this situation has become impossible. Tomorrow you will have to take your tadpole to the zoo."

"But I can't put my friend in a cage!" cried Louis.

That night Louis was very sad—until he remembered that the gym in the nearby high school had a swimming pool.

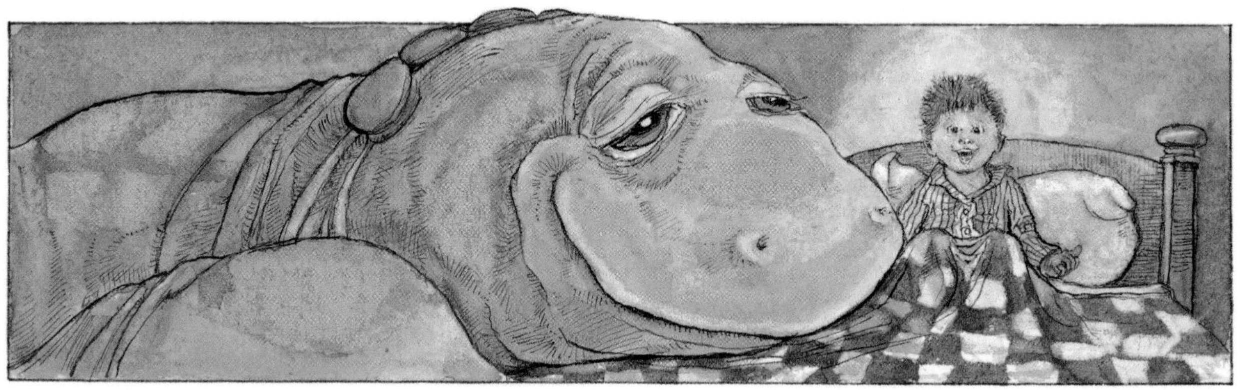

Louis hid Alphonse under a carpet and smuggled him inside.

"Nobody uses this place during the summer," whispered Louis. "You'll be safe here."

After making sure that Alphonse felt at home, Louis said good-bye. "I'll be back tomorrow with a big pile of cheeseburgers," he promised.

Louis came every afternoon to play with Alphonse. In the mornings he earned money for the cheeseburgers by delivering newspapers.

The training continued as well.
Louis would say, "Alphonse, RETRIEVE!"

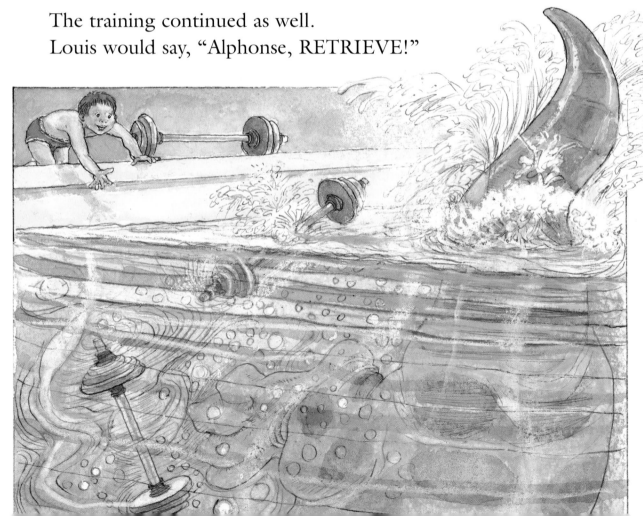

And Alphonse would succeed every time.

As summer vacation passed, Louis became more and more worried about what would happen to Alphonse when the high school kids returned.

After his first day of classes Louis ran to the high school, and found the gym bustling with activity. The swim team was heading for the pool.

"STOP!" cried Louis.

"On your mark!" bellowed the coach. "Get set!"
"Excuse me, sir," said Louis.

"GO!" roared the coach.

Alphonse rose to the surface to welcome the swimmers.

"It's a submarine from another planet!" shrieked the coach. "Call the police! Call the Navy!"

"No, it's only a tadpole," said Louis. "He's my pet."

The coach was upset and confused.

"You have until tomorrow," he cried, "to get that creature out of the pool!"

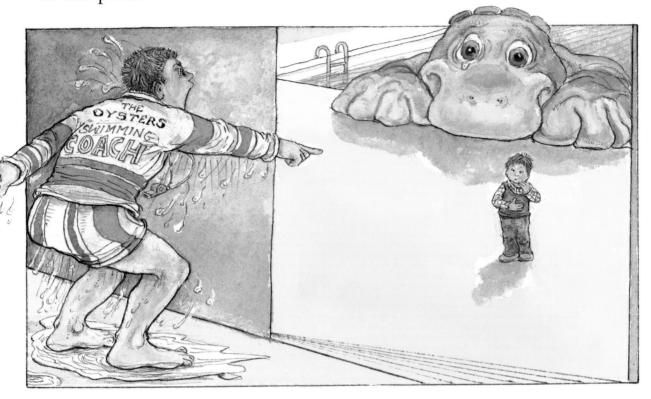

Louis telephoned his friend Ms. Seevers, the librarian, and asked for her help.

"I'll be right there!" she said.

Ms. Seevers rushed to meet Louis at the high school. When she saw Alphonse, she was so startled that she dropped her purse into the water.

"RETRIEVE!" said Louis. And Alphonse did.

"Where did this astounding animal come from?" cried Ms. Seevers.

"He was a birthday gift from my uncle," Louis replied.

Ms. Seevers telephoned Uncle McAllister.

"Oh, the wee tadpole?" he said. "Why, he came from the lake nearby. It's the one folks call Loch Ness."

"Brace yourself, Louis!" Ms. Seevers said. "I believe your uncle found the Loch Ness monster!"

"I don't care!" cried Louis. "Alphonse is my friend and I love him." He pleaded with Ms. Seevers to help him raise enough money to buy the parking lot so he could build a big swimming pool for Alphonse.

Suddenly Ms. Seevers had an idea. "Long ago a pirate ship sank in the harbor," she said. "No one has ever been able to find it—or its treasure chest. But perhaps we can!"

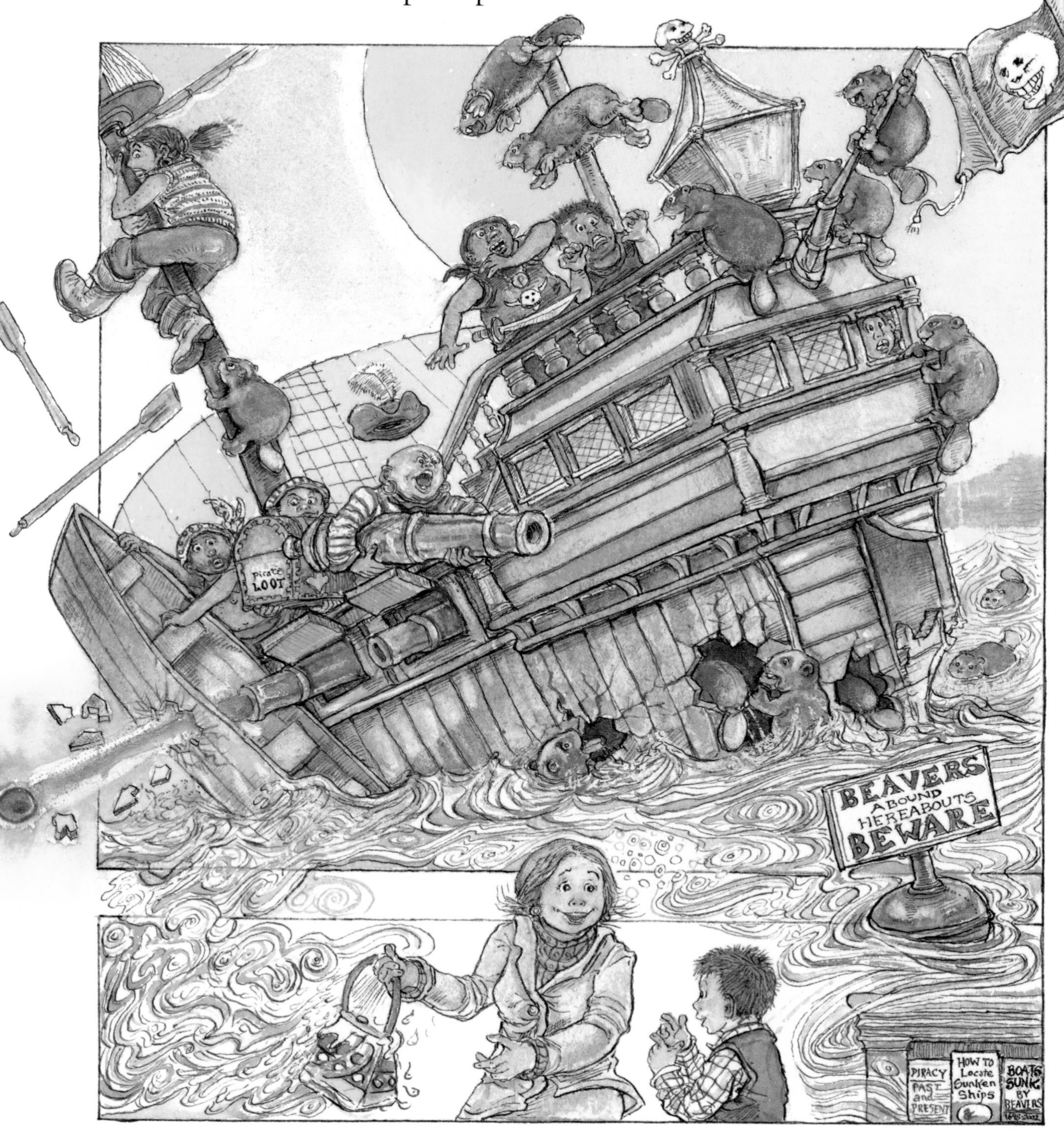

The next morning they drove to the harbor and rented a boat. "This is a treasure chest," cried Louis. "RETRIEVE!"

Alphonse disappeared under the water . . .

. . . and returned with the chest! It was filled with gold and jewels. “Let’s buy the parking lot and get to work!” cried Ms. Seevers.

Louis's parents were shocked to see a construction crew in the parking lot.

"Louis!" they cried. "What in the world is going on here?"

"Alphonse found a pirate treasure ship," explained Louis. "And we used part of our gold to buy you this present."

Louis's parents were shocked once again. "Tickets for a vacation cruise to Hawaii!" they gasped.

"And," said Louis, "you don't have to worry about us, because Granny has agreed to baby-sit."

They hugged Louis. They kissed Alphonse.

"How soon can we leave?" they cried.

"Immediately," said Louis.

By the time Louis's parents returned, the swimming pool was being enjoyed by everyone in the city.

I CAN SIT STAY and FETCH
HUFF AND PUFF
COACH

The Tadpole

A week later Louis said, "Alphonse, tomorrow is my birthday, which means that you've been my best friend for a whole year."

The next day Uncle McAllister arrived for the party.

"Greetings, Louis my lad!" he exclaimed. "I've come with a curious stone from the hills of Scotland. Happy birthday!"

"Wow! Thanks!" said Louis.

Suddenly the stone began to tremble and crack . . .

Born With a Crayon in His Hand

Born With a Crayon in His Hand

A Profile of Steven Kellogg

BY BARBARA ELLEMAN

When Steven Kellogg was a boy, he wanted a dog more than anything he could imagine—a dog he could run with, tussle with in the family's backyard in Darien, Connecticut, share his best secrets with, and enjoy as a day-by-day companion. Steven has fulfilled that wish several times over—owning, through the years, five enormous harlequin Great Danes and currently a taffy-colored cocker spaniel named Sylvia.

The childhood dream has been further realized in print: His book illustrations contain dogs big and small, rambunctious and mellow, playful and lazy. The Kellogg canines sometimes occupy center stage (*Pinkerton, Behave!*), or play supporting roles (*Best Friends*), while others work effectively as extras in crowd scenes (*Library Lil* and *Ralph's Secret Weapon*). Wherever they appear, their expressions and antics spice the pages with wit and humor. And, as his fans have come to expect, a Pinkerton image is tucked somewhere in almost every book.

The author-illustrator says he can't remember a time when he didn't want to make pictures. Born in 1941, Steven grew up during World War II and tells of drawing compulsively as a child. He laughingly says, "I think I was born with a picture in my head and a crayon in my hand." Often with his two sisters by his side, Steven would stack a pile of paper on his lap and scribble pictures while making up stories. If the tale was long, the floor would be covered with paper by the end of the session. They called it "telling stories on paper."

Left, Steven with a real-life Pinkerton
Above, Steven at approximately 14 months old
P. 325, Steven in Rome as a senior at RISD

"I drew my way through elementary school," Steven remembers. "Animals and birds were my favorite subjects." This obsession with pictures resulted in an ongoing need for supplies: He tried a lemonade-stand technique, offering pictures instead of drinks, and even attempted a door-to-door selling effort to generate cash. Lawn mowing and yard work proved more successful, however, and all profits were funneled into buying painting materials. Steven often pretended to be a *National Geographic* staff artist, on assignment to paint various animals around the world, using the magazine's photographs as models to guide his brush. "One of my ongoing projects was to draw every species of wildlife in the encyclopedia. Then I thumbtacked the pictures around my bedroom, changing the positioning over and over again whenever a new group was finished. I lived in a revolving world of wildlife," he says. "The wallpaper was ruined by the hundreds of holes; I don't think my parents ever forgot it."

Determined to pursue a career in art, despite lack of encouragement from his parents, Steven entered the Rhode Island School of Design in Providence, Rhode Island, on a Pitney Bowes full scholarship in 1959, majoring in illustration. The culmination—and highlight—of his RISD experience came in his senior year, when he was selected as recipient of a yearlong fellowship program in Florence, sailing steerage on an old steamer to Italy. The time there, he says, "cemented the notion that art would be my life's career."

After graduation, Kellogg moved to Washington, D.C., where he secured a

Left, a childhood drawing
Below, in his studio in Rome

Left to right: The Orchard Cat *cover; illustration from* Gwot!; *Steven and his wife, Helen (with Pinkerton); Steven with stepdaughters Pam, Kim, Laurie, and Melanie*

position teaching etching at American University. While thankful for the job, a bigger item on his agenda was fulfilling his great ambition—to write and illustrate children's books. He began sending manuscripts to publishers and received several appointments for a portfolio review. One, with Ursula Nordstrom at Harper and Row, resulted in his first assignment: the now long-out-of-print title *Gwot! Horribly Funny Hairticklers* by George Mendoza. Three years later, his dream of illustrating his own stories was finally realized with the publication of *The Wicked Kings of Bloon*, followed shortly by *The Orchard Cat*. This tale about a pompous cat who, with the help of a caring young boy, becomes a changed feline had a positive reception from children and critics. Kellogg the author and illustrator was on his way to fulfilling his dream.

Another life-changing event occurred when Steven met and married a widow with six children. They purchased an eighteenth-century farmhouse beside a small brook in Sandy Hook, Connecticut. Helen, Steven's wife, is an authority on early American folk artists, and their house reflected this joint interest. Old-fashioned rockers, four-poster beds, antique toys, and primitive paintings brought a warm ambiance to their home. When the children were growing up, Steven says, "the house trembled at times, but it was a generous, welcoming old place with six bedrooms on the second floor and two bedrooms on the third

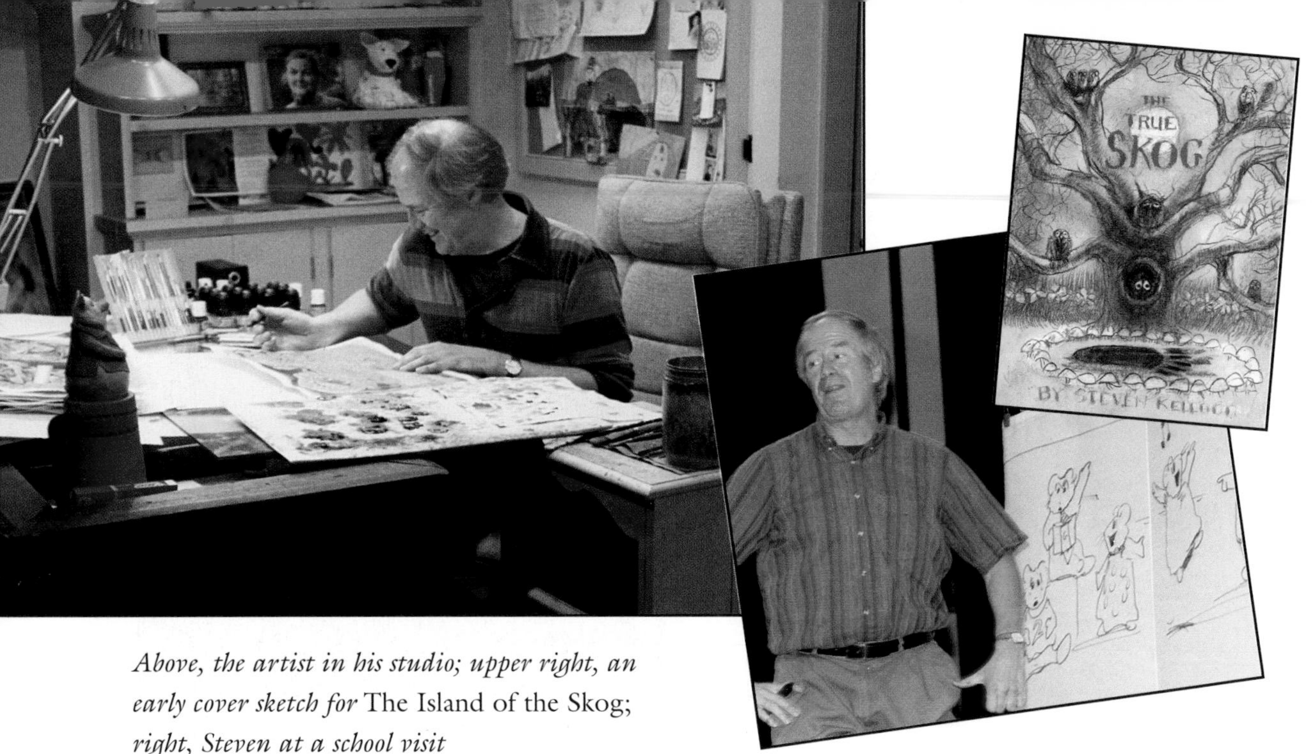

Above, the artist in his studio; upper right, an early cover sketch for The Island of the Skog; *right, Steven at a school visit*

floor, which tended to absorb the crowd." He describes his family life as a wonderful adventure.

However, when southern Connecticut began to aggressively suburbanize, the Kelloggs decided to move north. Already owning a summer home, an Adirondack camp in upstate New York, they bought a winterized historic house on Lake Champlain and have made it their full-time residence. A breathtaking view, down a steep hill and across the lake, awaits Kellogg from his barn studio, and helps to nudge forth the creative muse. And just like that child of long ago, his drawing board is still where the illustrator loves to be.

It was from this very drawing board that early blockbuster titles such as *Can I Keep Him?,* his most autobiographical tale, were conceived and created. Steven's penchant for centering his stories on animals continued with such tales as the well-loved *The Mysterious Tadpole.* Originally produced with the 1977 limitations of pre-separated art, the book was recently re-illustrated in full color for its twenty-fifth anniversary, bringing heightened expressivity to the story.

Another popular book featuring animals is *The Island of the Skog,* which has continued to play an important role in Kellogg's life. Thousands of children, librarians, and teachers across the country have been treated to a dramatic reading and visual presentation of the story. Several times a month, Kellogg climbs aboard an airplane and flies off to visit schools. Upon arrival, he sets up his three-by-five-foot drawing board and, felt-tipped pen in hand, proceeds to tell *The Island of the Skog.* With a voice that changes from a whisper to a boom, he unfolds his tale. At appropriate points, he rips pages with great flair off the drawing pad. By the end of the session, the floor is a swirl of litter—reminiscent of the author's early drawing days with his sisters. Then, with the teacher and children still marveling over the gift of his drawings, Kellogg is on his way to enchant another waiting audience.

While many illustrators of his stature have long since given up visiting schools, Kellogg feels it is necessary to keep in touch with children. "I find that an ongoing exposure to children informs and enhances my writing and illustrating, and keeps an awareness of my audience for the book fresh and vibrant."

One immediately senses this awareness of children when inspecting the parade of youngsters who pepper Kellogg's artwork: Clothes in disarray, shoelaces untied, and hair askew, they elicit a range of emotions in tandem with the stories in which they appear. Color-drenched pages with swirling lines of action are signature Kellogg, as are the imaginative high jinks that propel so many of his stories (such as *Won't Somebody Play with Me?* and *Much Bigger Than Martin*).

As Steven's success grew, the residents of Sandy Hook became used to having a celebrity in their midst—and to seeing

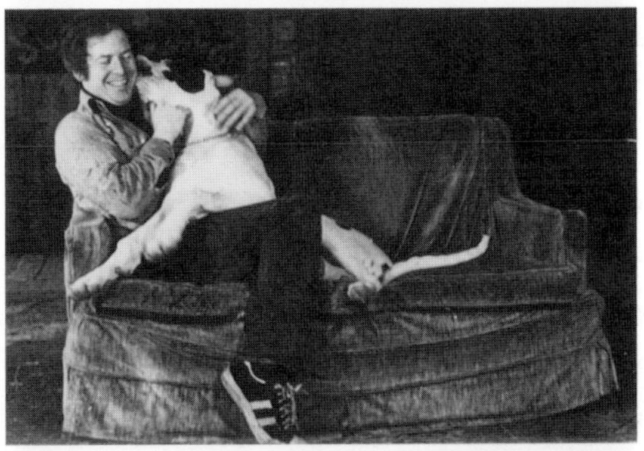

Steven with Pinkerton

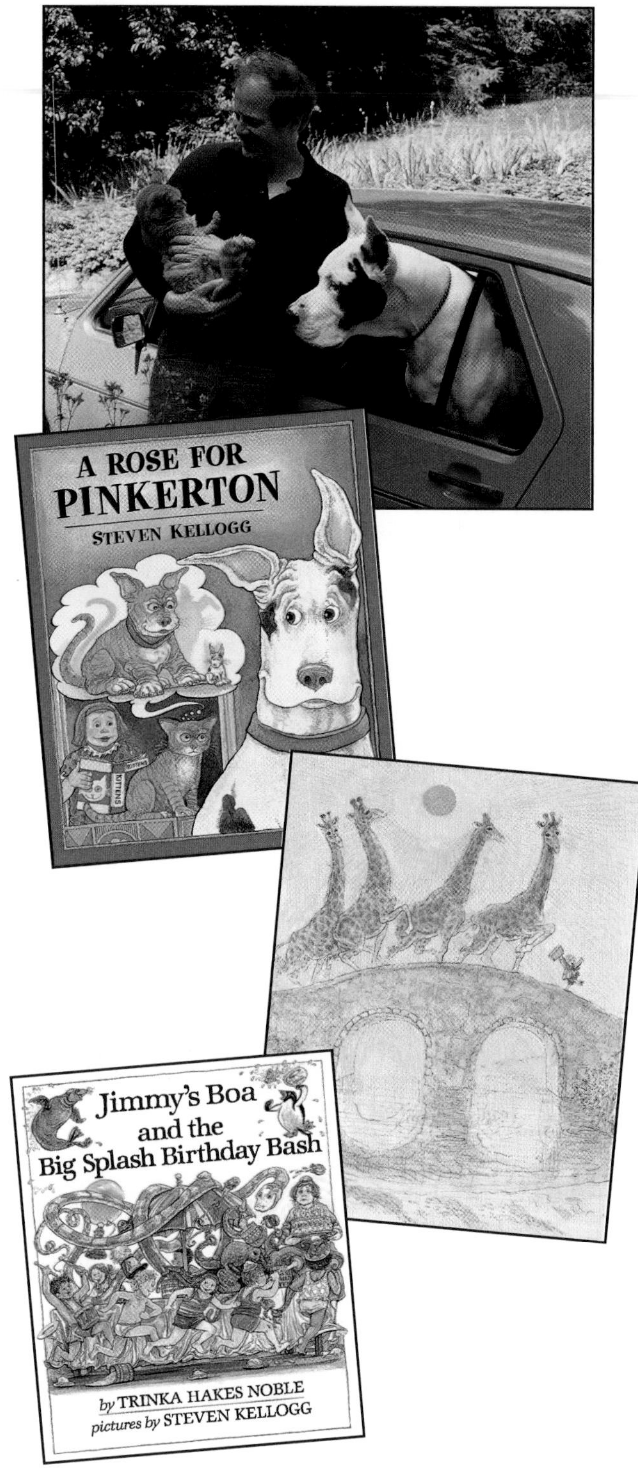

Top to bottom: Steven with Secondhand Rose and Pinkerton; book cover; illustration from The Boy Who Was Followed Home*; book cover*

the head of a huge 180-pound harlequin Great Dane protruding out of the sunroof of Steven's small car. "As a pup," Kellogg recalls, "Pinkerton was extremely challenging; his puppyhood extended far beyond the time frame that is considered normal. We were alternately driven wild by his stubborn inadaptability and seduced by his irresistible charm. Our efforts to deal with his baffling contradictions inspired *Pinkerton, Behave!*"

As the years passed, Pinkerton's continuing antics motivated the author to create sequels entitled *A Rose for Pinkerton; Tallyho, Pinkerton!; Prehistoric Pinkerton;* and, most recently, *A Penguin Pup for Pinkerton.*

The inspiration for the heroine of *A Rose for Pinkerton* was an assertive, independent cat named Secondhand Rose. According to Steven, she was born wild in the Catskill Mountains, adopted as a kitten by the Kellogg family, and then devoted the rest of her long life to harassing Pinkerton. Although in the book Pinkerton and Rose become friends, in real life, the author says, the two never tired of finding ways to make each other miserable.

In addition to the books Steven has written and illustrated, he also has collaborated with other writers; notably Margaret Mahy (*The Boy Who Was Followed Home* and *The Rattlebang Picnic*), Suzanne Williams (*Library Lil*),

Trinka Hakes Noble, Deborah Guarino, Amy Ehrlich, David Schwartz, and Reeve Lindbergh.

The Noble collaboration has been hugely successful: *The Day Jimmy's Boa Ate the Wash, Jimmy's Boa Bounces Back,* and *Jimmy's Boa and the Big Splash Birthday Bash* are staples in classrooms and libraries. A fourth title, *Jimmy's Boa and the Bungee Jump Slam Dunk,* continues the saga of a lovable boa who simply can't stay out of trouble. Noble and Kellogg's first effort had an interesting beginning. When Kellogg was approached to do the illustrations, he told the editor that he liked the story but felt the title, *Our Class Trip to the Farm,* needed perking up. The editor agreed and contacted Noble about Kellogg's suggestion—*The Day Jimmy's Boa Ate the Wash.* The author loved the new title, as did readers; *Newsweek* called it "the best title of the year."

Visual storytelling is a natural part of a Kellogg production, which often starts before the text begins and ends after the tale closes. This is highly evident in *The Day Jimmy's Boa Ate the Wash.* The scene is set on the half-title page with a clutch of children boisterously piling off the bus, and brought to conclusion after the text ends, in a picture of the sweatered boa snuggling happily into life at the farm. This kind of tongue-in-cheek image, providing a final exclamation mark to the story, is another Kellogg trademark.

Evidence of Kellogg's artistic cleverness abounds in Reeve Lindbergh's *The Day the Goose Got Loose,* where the havoc one large domestic goose creates on an autumn day when wild geese fly south is fortified by a layout that propels the action and suspense forward. Another highly successful partnership was with Deborah Guarino for *Is Your Mama a Llama?* Aimed at very young readers—and turned into a board book—the story's minimal text is bolstered by bucolic landscapes and endearing animal

Illustrations from
The Day the Goose Got Loose

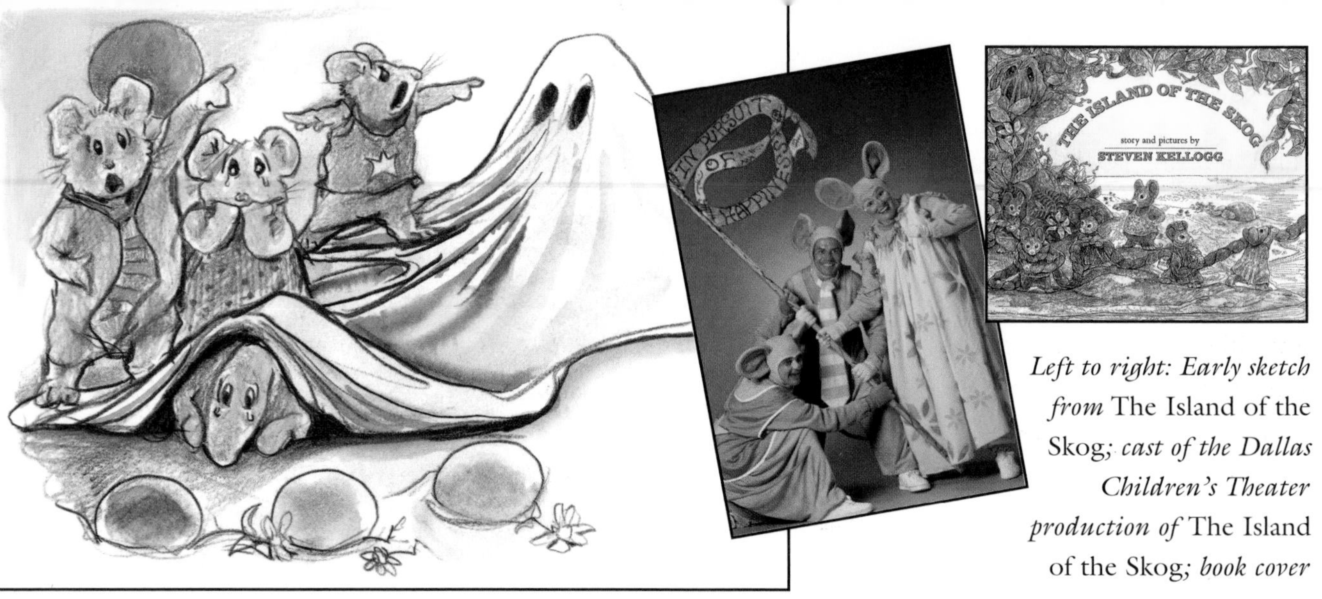
THE ISLAND OF THE SKOG
story and pictures by
STEVEN KELLOGG

Left to right: Early sketch from The Island of the Skog; *cast of the Dallas Children's Theater production of* The Island of the Skog; *book cover*

portrayals that maintain their animal nature.

How Much is a Million?, *If You Made a Million*, and *Millions to Measure*, all by David Schwartz, represent Kellogg's foray into nonfiction. Expanding on Schwartz's texts, he turns these concept books into fun adventures led by Marvelosissimo the Mathematical Magician.

Always a lover and appreciator of American folktales, Kellogg created a series of picture books especially for young readers. Existing editions at the time, Kellogg felt, were heavy on text and shy on illustration, and he wanted to give younger children a taste of Americana. "The tall tale is American mythology, and part of our national character, which expressed itself by concocting larger-than-life heroes who share an outrageous sense of humor, outlandish proportions, and an eagerness to tackle immense challenges." Exaggeration being Kellogg's forte, Paul Bunyan was a perfect first choice. Success spawned tales of folk heroes such as Pecos Bill, Johnny Appleseed, Mike Fink, and Sally Ann Thunder Ann Whirlwind Crockett.

Two stories close to Steven Kellogg's heart are *Best Friends* and *The Christmas Witch*. Both offer themes he finds important: friendship and a belief in doing one's best. In 1995, *The Christmas Witch* was adapted by Linda Daugherty for the Dallas Children's Theater and was applauded so highly that it was staged again in 1997. Six years later the troupe opened a new state-of-the-art theater with a revival of their production of *The Island of the Skog*, which the theater had previously sent on a sixty-city tour.

It isn't surprising that theaters want to adapt Kellogg's stories, as they are ripe with movement, action, and well-defined characters. When asked which comes first, the story or the pictures, Kellogg replies: "When I am both the author and the illustrator, I find that the two components tend to spring to life simultaneously in the form of fragmented series of images with words attached. They are like little pieces of film with sound, and I often feel like a film editor as I splice some sequences together and cut others, trying countless combinations to find the most effective movement for the book."

He also compares the picture book to the stage, saying that an unread book is like a darkened theater. That theater is illuminated when the book is opened, and the carefully orchestrated turning of the page is like the curtain rising on successive acts and scenes, propelling the reader and observer into the evolving movement of the story. Kellogg, an ardent theater and opera fan, makes dynamic use of entrances and exits for his characters, supplies careful "set design" and costuming, and structures believable beginnings and endings—surely a benefit from his years of theatergoing.

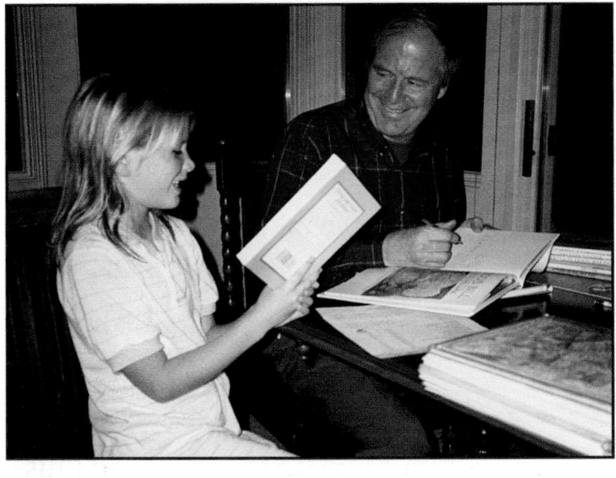

Steven with his granddaughter Amy

He combines these skills with an unfailing sense of humor. Kellogg's readers have come to expect laughs from his playful characters, exaggerated fun, jovial situations, and injected details. Recognition of his ability to provide humor that is neither too banal nor too sophisticated came with the 1998 Jo Osborne Award for humor in children's books, presented by the Ohio Library Foundation. Kellogg also received the 1987 David McCord Citation, the 1989 Regina Medal from the Catholic Library Association, and the Rhode Island School of Design Alumni Award for Significant Professional Achievement—all recognizing his outstanding contribution to children's literature.

Asked about his favorite book, he claims that is like trying to name a favorite child: "Creating a book is like making a friend. Each relationship with a friend is different and unique, and that is what I feel about my books." As to which book represents his greatest artistic challenge, Kellogg speaks of the eighteen paintings he provided for a Books of Wonder edition of Mark Twain's *Huckleberry Finn*. "It was especially challenging because it is not a picture book but a monumental novel." The original paintings are larger than seen in the book. Although Kellogg usually illustrates in the same size as the book page—he feels it is necessary to work with images as they will appear in relation to the typography and the young reader's vision—*Huckleberry Finn* demanded another approach. "It was a privilege," he says, "to be immersed for many months in the power, the beauty, and the humor of Twain's magnificent writing."

His calendar filled with publisher due dates, speaking engagements, author tours, and school visits, does Steven Kellogg think of slowing down? "I think of it all the time," he says, "but then the momentum just happily continues." A combination of mischief and glee tug his mouth into a smile. "Actually, I think I'm getting away with something—to spend every day doing what I enjoy, and be able to do it for a living. When I talk with children they often ask if I like what I do. It's great to be able to say that I love my work."

Steven's exuberance continues to translate stories to pictures to page; two much anticipated books on his drawing board are *Santa Claus Is Coming to Town* and *The Pied Piper of Hamlin.* A constant advocate of reading, he urges parents, teachers, and librarians to motivate young readers by enthusiastically recommending and sharing books as if each story is a treasured gift. And gifts are what Steven Kellogg gives readers each time he sits down at his drawing board to sketch out the misadventures of a beguiling boa, mice sailing off in search of safe harbor, a tadpole of amazing origins, or that clumsy, huggable Great Dane named Pinkerton.

Steven with Goldensilverwind the cocker spaniel,
who was named for the puppy in Best Friends

Price James Memorial Library
212707